"Are you going to hurt Simon?"

"I thought you and Max were worried about him hurting me," Wynne replied. "Was that just hype to get me interested in him?"

Becca sat up. "No, no. I was concerned, but now I see how vulnerable he is. And you're so driven, Wynne. Your career is everything. Can you imagine living on Eagle Island and not going off on a new adventure?"

"For the first time I'm actually considering what that might be like," Wynne admitted in a low voice. "The thought of leaving for Australia isn't very attractive, and I was really excited before I came here." Was she losing her drive? Had meeting Simon changed her that much?

Her sister went silent at her admission. Then she cleared her throat. "You've got it bad, big sister," she said softly.

Becca wasn't telling Wynne anything she wasn't already beginning to suspect.

Books by Colleen Rhoads

Love Inspired Suspense

**Windigo Twilight* #3
**Shadow Bones* #9
**Stormcatcher* #16

*Great Lakes Legends

COLLEEN RHOADS

loves to convey the compelling truth of God's love and grace through her fiction. Colleen and her husband reside in Indiana when they're not traveling the globe looking for new adventures to write about. She loves to hear from her readers! You can e-mail her at colleencoble@comcast.net.

STORMCATCHER

COLLEEN RHOADS

Published by Steeple Hill Books™

STEEPLE HILL BOOKS

ISBN 0-373-87348-4

STORMCATCHER

This edition published by arrangement with Steeple Hill Books.

www.SteepleHill.com

Printed in U.S.A.

Of what use is money in the hand of a fool,
since he has no desire to get wisdom?
—*Proverbs* 17:16

For my critique partners and wonderful friends,
Kristin Billerbeck, Denise Hunter and Diann Hunt

PROLOGUE

Grinning, Corbin Griswall whirled his reel and ran his line in, fighting the heavy pull on the other end. It had been a slow day for fishing, and the two small crappies he'd caught hadn't put up this much of a struggle. He was panting by the time the object surfaced. Corbin started at the realization that it wasn't a salmon he'd landed.

A man, perfectly preserved by Superior's cold water. He either hadn't been dead long enough for the fish to feed on him, or he'd been enclosed in a boat where they couldn't get to him. Corbin thought of the old Gordon Lightfoot song about Superior never giving up her dead. She'd probably released this poor soul reluctantly in last night's storm.

He reached for his thermos. Coffee would help him wake up before he called the Coast Guard. He was already planning how to regale his buddies with the tale in Turtle Town.

ONE

"Sounds like she's ready to eat." Wynne Baxter shifted baby Isabelle from one shoulder to the other as the infant made tiny mewling noises and stuck her fist in her mouth.

The noise did funny things to her insides—Wynne felt as soft as a marshmallow at the feel of her tiny niece. She marveled at the helplessness of the tiny limbs and the screwed-up face that was a perfect replica of her sister Becca.

Becca smiled and held out her arms. "It's past time." She cradled the baby in her arms and settled herself on the sofa to nurse her.

Wynne watched her sister, amazed at the transformation over the past year. Becca had blossomed under Max's love and care. The baby snatched a lock of blond hair in her tiny fingers and gave a grunt of contentment. She burrowed deeply against her mother.

"You act like you've been a mother forever," Wynne

told her. She heard the note of envy in her voice. Some days she wondered what she'd missed by her obsession with old ships.

Since she was a little girl she'd been fascinated with tales of pirate ships, of clipper ships plying the waters off Boston, of the great discoveries of Columbus. Stories like that held her in thrall, and she'd translated that passion into her life's work.

The work felt paltry and worthless when she looked at her niece.

Becca glanced up. "Your turn will come soon enough."

Wynne didn't want to go there. Give Becca an inch and she'd be calling all the eligible bachelors on the island. "I don't know what I'm going to do with myself all summer. I'm enjoying the time with you and Jake, but I'm not used to just sitting around."

"I was thinking about that," Becca admitted. "Have you ever thought of doing some searching in Lake Superior?"

Wynne stopped swinging her foot back and forth. "You think there are some wrecks close to the island?" She knew there were wrecks in Lake Superior, but the thought of searching there hadn't crossed her mind.

"I'm sure of it. There are dozens of schooners lost in the lake, and their whereabouts are unknown. You might find something really important. One of the most hotly sought ships is the *Merchant.* Someone claimed to have spotted her masts thirty feet below the surface in the Grand Island area, but she's never been located."

Wynne knew she should be content to spend time with her family for the summer until her new project in Australia started in the fall, but the prospect of three months of inactivity took its toll on her spirits. Her mind danced with visions of a century-old schooner, masts still intact, and wonderfully preserved by Superior's cold water.

Becca must have caught Wynne's fascination because she chuckled. "You marine archaeologists are all alike," she teased.

Wynne returned her smile. "I'll have to check into it," she said. "Do you think I could find a boat to rent?"

Becca put Isabelle over her shoulder and patted her back. "Max's best friend, Simon Lassiter, has just the boat you need. He's even got sonar equipment on board."

Sonar wasn't common equipment. "Why would he have a boat all decked out for deep water searches?"

"He's been searching for Viking longboats for ten years. He's convinced the Vikings made it this far, and that the remains of a boat is out there somewhere just waiting to be found. And it helps that he's part owner of a yacht building company."

"And this crackpot is Max's best friend?" A memory teased the edges of Wynne's thoughts. The name sounded vaguely familiar. "Is he some old codger with more money than brains?"

Becca bit her lip, but the smile she was trying to hide broke through. "I think I'll let you discover that for yourself. He's coming to dinner tonight. You can ask him about his boat then."

For one, horrifying moment, Wynne thought her sister might be matchmaking, then she dismissed the ridiculous thought. Becca knew better than to try to hook her up with a fool. Her sister knew Wynne didn't tolerate idiotic science. And believing a Viking ship had made it this far inland was as idiotic an idea as they came.

She smiled. "I'll try to keep my cool long enough to sweet-talk him into taking me out on the water. This summer might turn out to be fun after all."

"What is Isabelle, chopped liver?" Becca deposited the sleeping infant into Wynne's arms. "Here, enjoy your niece and quit thinking about leaving us."

Simon Lassiter guided his yacht to the Windigo Manor dock. While he enjoyed Max Duncan's company, he had a feeling there was more to tonight's invitation than the discussion of football and hockey over coffee in the living room. Max had been much too casual when he mentioned his sister-in-law, Wynne Baxter, would be there as well.

After years of escaping the clutches of matchmaking mamas, Simon could sniff out romantic intent like a lynx on a rabbit trail. In Simon's experience, most women were interested in his money, not in him. Maybe he was too cynical and saw dollar signs in a woman's eyes, but he'd been burned too many times. And since his fiancée, Amanda, had betrayed him, his cynicism had deepened.

He thought he might have met Wynne when they

were kids. The name sounded familiar. He looped the rope around the piling and stepped onto the dock. Max had given the weathered wood a new coat of paint, he noticed.

He lifted his face to the dying light. The early June sunshine had softened to the gentle quality of late afternoon illumination that bathed the world in a warm glow. With an evening like this, it was hard to let even a possible matchmaking situation bother him.

He flicked a bug from his otherwise impeccably clean khaki trousers and bounded up the hill to the house.

Max answered before Simon had a chance to rap on the door. "Hey, buddy, right on time."

"You sound surprised. I'm never late." Simon stepped onto the oak floors inside the house.

Windigo Manor never failed to enthrall him. The ornate woodwork and thick plaster walls had weathered storms both inside and out. History no one would fully know had played out inside these ten thousand square feet. Sometimes, Simon imagined he heard the echo of voices from another time and wished he could eavesdrop on the life lived here a hundred years ago.

Max clapped him on the shoulder, and Simon noticed a spot on his friend's shirt. "Looks like the princess couldn't quite keep her milk down."

Max glanced at the wet stain. "Trust you to notice. You'll likely have one of your own before the night is out."

Not if Simon could help it. Infants terrified him. The

Was that mockery on her face? He could only hope and pray she never told anyone what she'd seen. Max would never let him live it down. "I have an opening on my team right now for a chef." His grin broadened, knowing she would refuse.

One dark brow lifted. "Oh dear, I hope your crew has a penchant for peanut butter sandwiches and chips. I'll take it."

His smile faltered, and his gaze connected with Max's. His buddy shrugged and grinned. "Wynne is always up for a challenge. I hope your crew has cast-iron stomachs. I've sampled her cooking."

His wife elbowed him. "Wynne is a good cook."

Wynne burst out laughing. "Only a sister could call that concoction I fixed last night good. You know how our housekeeper can be. Moxie will be horrified when she gets back tomorrow and sees the remains in the refrigerator. But I'm game if Simon is."

Her gaze challenged him. "Why am I suddenly afraid?" He couldn't help it. He liked her spirit. His cell phone chirped, and he dragged it out. "Lassiter," he said.

He recognized the new sheriff's voice. There was no trace of warmth in Mitch Rooney's voice. "Simon, Jerry has been found."

Simon's muscles tightened. He had something to say to his cousin when they met. Though in hindsight he knew he and Amanda were wrong for each other, he'd never expected Jerry to try to come between them. "Where is he?"

"In the morgue. A fisherman snagged his body."

"His body—wait. You mean he's dead?" Simon sank into a chair. He pressed his fingers against his eyes. Jerry couldn't be dead.

"Didn't you at least suspect he was dead?" Rooney's cynicism was showing.

"He'd taken off like this before. I thought he and Amanda—" Simon broke off. He'd been sure Jerry had taken off with Amanda, and they would both show up sooner or later. They'd been gone three months.

"Last night's storm must have released him from the boat or wherever he'd been trapped," Rooney said.

Simon's stomach was clenched. "Have you called Brian?"

"Not yet. I thought you might want to tell him."

At least the sheriff was showing a bit of compassion. Simon didn't like the suspicion he felt radiating through the phone. There was no love lost between him and Rooney.

"I'll go there now." Simon clicked off the phone and turned to his host. Max was looking worried.

"Jerry?" Max said.

Simon nodded. "Jerry's dead. They found his body. I have to go tell Brian."

"You doing okay? Want me to come with you?"

A wave of grief engulfed Simon. His cousin had been as close as a brother. He shook his head. "I'd better do this alone." Jerry's brother, Brian, was a private person. He wouldn't want anyone but family to see his grief.

Max nodded. "Call if you need anything." He squeezed Simon's shoulder then dropped his hand.

Simon nodded. His throat felt tight. "I need to find the boat, figure out what happened. It was to be our flagship, a yacht that would change the world. Brian and I need to determine what went wrong."

Wynne watched Simon's broad-shouldered form jog down the hill to the waiting yacht. Seeing him again brought back memories of her childhood. And the crush she'd had on him.

She let the curtain fall back into place and turned back to look at her sister. "Tell me what's going on," she said to her sister.

Becca took the baby and began to rock her. "Simon's partner and cousin, Jerry Lassiter, took out a new prototype yacht they'd built. Jerry insisted on taking it out alone because it was supposed to be completely automated where one man could handle it, in spite of its size. That was three months ago. He never came back."

"Didn't anyone try to find him?" Wynne asked.

"When Simon's fiancée, Amanda, went missing as well, we assumed the two had run off together. Jerry had done that once before with his brother's girlfriend. From what I hear, Jerry liked what he couldn't have. He could sweet-talk an oyster into giving up its pearl."

"No one thought of a tragedy?" Wynne asked. "That's an expensive boat. They would have wanted to salvage what they could. And collect the insurance."

Becca shook her head. “It was a beautiful summer day. Light breeze, blue skies. No reason for the boat to be in danger. Simon checked different ports but no one had seen them. Everyone assumed it was just Jerry pulling another of his stunts. We all thought he’d be back when he was ready. He’d done it before, and he was the primary owner of the business. Simon just dabbles for fun. He was left a boatload of money by his parents.”

“Still, I would have thought they would have looked for a wreck.”

“I think the old sheriff did a cursory flyover of the area, but when nothing turned up, we all assumed he’d return when he was ready,” Becca said. “Maybe he’d made it to port somewhere and garaged it.”

“No wonder Simon was upset. Does he still think Amanda was with him? Maybe she’s dead, too.”

“Maybe. I’m sure the sheriff will figure it out,” Max said. “Now what was all that shared history about? I take it you knew him as a kid?”

Wynne knew Simon wouldn’t want her blabbing. “I had a fearsome crush on him when I was a kid, like twelve or thirteen. He was five years older than me so I was just in the way.” Remembering the way she’d chased after him made her face burn. How childish.

“What was his nickname?” Max smiled as his daughter cooed.

Wynne shook her head. “I think he wouldn’t want me to say.”

“Since when does that stop you?” Becca said. She

handed the baby to Max. "Are you really going to hire on as cook?"

Wynne smiled. "I think he was kidding, but I might do it if he's serious. You think I'm nuts?"

"You always do the unexpected." Becca handed her daughter a rattle. "But watch out. Simon has broken more hearts than I can count."

"Hey, not on purpose," Max protested. "He never tries to attract them. But he's a good-looking guy."

"And he has money," Becca added. "A lethal combination."

"My heart is safe," Wynne assured them. "I'm not missing this new project for anyone. I had to fight tooth and nail for my spot."

"Oh? Did it get vicious?" Becca's eyes were avid with curiosity.

"You might say that." Wynne didn't like to think about it. Pain squeezed her lungs.

"Did you call Jackson back?" Becca asked.

Her sister must have read her mind. Wynne shook her head. "I have nothing more to say to him."

"He called twice yesterday."

"Just tell him I don't want to talk to him." If she ever saw Jackson Country again, it would be too soon. He'd tried to torpedo her career once too often. She wouldn't put it past him to take her place on this new project even now. Once their romance was over, it was as if he was determined to bury her and any shred of her reputation.

TWO

The boatyard was deserted except for Brian's blue truck. Simon skirted several yachts in various stages of construction. He followed the sound of the hammer and the smell of sawdust. He found his cousin pounding nails into a prop under a yacht that looked nearly finished.

The back of Brian's blue chambray shirt was soaked with perspiration. He was two years younger than Simon, and people often thought Simon, Jerry and Brian were brothers instead of cousins. They had the Lassiter broad shoulders and long legs. Brian's hair was a shade lighter than Jerry's and Simon's, but the three had the same shaped nose and cleft chin.

On Brian it had always seemed weak and ineffectual. Jerry had been the best-looking of the three, but if Brian had noticed, he'd never shown he minded the way women threw themselves at his brother and looked right past him. The whole family had always been in Jerry's thrall.

Simon stood and watched him for a moment. He

dreaded telling his cousin the news. The two of them were all that were left of the younger Lassiters now. Simon was an only child, and now Brian had no siblings as well. Simon still couldn't believe it.

Brian paused to wipe his forehead and saw Simon. The welcoming smile faltered as he took in his cousin's expression. "What's wrong?" Brian laid down the hammer and came toward him.

Simon forced the words out. "It's Jerry. He's been found."

Brian's dark eyes widened. "Found? He's back on the island or still off partying?"

Stupid. He should have watched his words. Simon shook his head. "No, I'm sorry, I'm not being clear. His body has been found. The sheriff just called me."

Brian flinched. He dropped his head. "No." He backed away. "He's not dead!"

"I'm sorry, Brian." Simon swallowed the lump that had formed like a boulder in his throat. He put his hand on his cousin's shoulder.

Brian's eyes shimmered with moisture. He wiped his hand over his forehead. "And the boat?"

"No sign of it. The storm probably shook Jerry's body loose." He squeezed Brian's shoulder. "I'm sorry. I thought for sure he'd show up when he was ready."

Brian pounded his fist against the wooden hull. He pinched the bridge of his nose and visibly struggled for control.

Simon wanted to comfort him but didn't know how. "You okay?" he muttered, ill at ease.

Brian took a deep breath. "Thanks, Simon. Jerry was always so full of life. I just didn't want to believe he could die." His voice was low. "I guess I have to go identify the body."

"I'll go with you," Simon said.

Brian shook his head. "I'll be fine. Thanks for being the one to break the news."

"No problem. If you need to talk later, call me." He knew Brian wouldn't call though. His cousin was a private man and kept his problems to himself.

Brian nodded. "I'd better call the sheriff and find out where he wants to meet." He went to the building.

Simon watched him, shoulders slumped and his steps slow, as he went up the steps and inside. He clenched his hands. If only there was something he could do. His cousins had looked up to him for guidance all their lives, and it felt wrong to be bereft of any possibility of fixing things.

There was one thing he could do. He could find the yacht that carried Jerry to his cold grave and figure out what went wrong. Brian could carry on here at the shipyard for a while without him. He could work on finding the *Superior Lady* in the day.

His flagging spirits rose at the thought of action. He jogged to his boat and fired up the engine. His first stop would be to talk to the sheriff about where Jerry's body had been found.

The light was dying in the west, letting a cool breeze waft through its gold and red fingers. Goosebumps rose on Wynne's arms, and she rubbed them. She and her sister sat on the porch swing, the silence between them comfortable.

Through the open window, the TV blared as Molly, Max's 6-year-old daughter from his first marriage, watched a family comedy with her father. The baby was asleep, and this time with her sister felt as precious as a Spanish doubloon.

Becca broke the silence. "What did you think of Simon?"

"What's that supposed to mean?" Wynne looked her sister in the face. "Are you matchmaking?"

Becca's face took on an innocence. "Who, me? Of course not. But Max might be."

Wynne laughed, and kicked the swing into motion with her bare foot. "Simon seemed eager to get away from me. Maybe he thinks I'm still mooning over him. It might be interesting to look for some shipwrecks out there. Though I don't think we're going to find any Viking ship."

"Probably not," Becca agreed. "Max and I think the world of Simon. You could do worse."

"You're like a tenacious crab. I'm not interested in Simon."

"Did someone mention my name?" Simon materialized from the deepening shadows in the front yard.

Wynne nearly climbed up the porch railing. "You scared the life out of me! I didn't hear your truck."

He grinned, his teeth shining white in the dim light. "Sorry. I walked. Is Max around? I need to talk to him."

"He's watching TV with Molly."

Becca waited until Simon was inside the house. "Wonder what he wants? It didn't seem like a social call."

Wynne shrugged. "Maybe he's found Atlantis or something."

Her sister yanked on Wynne's braid. "He's not that crazy."

"You couldn't convince me," Wynne said, following her into the house. "Maybe it's about his cousin."

"Maybe," Becca said.

"Did you know Amanda?" Wynne had been curious about the woman Simon had chosen. She couldn't imagine someone throwing a man like Simon away. But maybe his cousin Jerry had been an exceptional man, too.

"Yeah."

"You sound less than enamored of her." Now Wynne was really curious. Becca liked everyone.

"Let's just say she always seemed to be looking out for herself."

"How did you know her?"

"She and I use the same hairdresser."

"Well, how unusual when there are only two on the island," Wynne teased. "Did you ever talk to her?"

"Once or twice. All she ever wanted to talk about was fashion and jewelry. She flashed around that fancy ring Simon bought her and talked about the big house they were going to build. It was pretty obvious money was all-important to her."

"Simon seems too smart to have let himself be caught by a money monger."

"She was good at covering it with me. I saw her in the café a time or two with Simon, and she was as sweet as pie. Kind to the waitress, that sort of thing. She knew how to work men."

"I wonder how long it would have taken Simon to see through her?"

"Men can be so blind when a beautiful woman is involved."

"Is that a trace of bitterness I hear?" Wynne asked, laughing.

"Well, you have to admit that men weren't beating down my door."

"Only because you hid your beauty."

"At my height, I wasn't hiding anything," Becca said dryly.

"At least Max was clever enough to recognize how smart and truly lovely you are."

"Spoken like a loyal sister," Becca said, laughing.

"Do you sometimes pinch yourself when you think of how your life has changed?" Wynne couldn't hide the wistful tone in her voice. She was thrilled her sister and brother were happily settled, but sometimes she felt like she was in the dark looking into a warmly lit house.

Becca stretched. "It's like a dream world. I'm so happy. Sometimes I wake up in the night and just watch Max sleeping. I listen to Isabelle on the baby monitor and know all is right with my world. God is so good."

"Yes, He is," Wynne agreed. It felt like lip service though. She'd given God so little thought lately. She knew she needed to find a better balance with her life, but it was hard not to let busyness take over.

"You sound a little glum."

"Just a little introspective." Wynne forced a smile. "What do you think happened to *Superior Lady?* Simon seemed shocked it could have sunk."

"I am, too. It was a great boat. Max wanted to have one like it built."

"I suppose the sheriff will figure it out." Wynne frowned when she remembered the tension in Simon's voice when he talked to the sheriff.

"Oh, Mitch Rooney will be pursuing it hard and heavy." Becca's voice was grim.

"What do you mean?"

"He has a personal stake in it. But I'd rather not talk about that. We've gossiped enough, I'm going to have to repent as it is."

"Do you think he suspects foul play?" Wynne hadn't thought of that possibility until now. She moved uneasily.

"Oh, no, surely not."

Her sister's tone didn't sound all that convincing. Would Simon be a suspect if Jerry's death was deemed a homicide? Wynne knew it was a stupid thought. Of course he would. Someone close to the victim was always considered the first suspect to look at.

Who really knew what lay behind another person's smile? Over the years, Wynne had found the people you were most prone to trust were often the very ones who stabbed you in the back.

But murder was a different story.

"I don't think Simon would kill anyone," she said.

"You sound like you know him pretty well. What's your history with him? You said you had a crush on him? Did you spend much time with him?"

"I followed him around for four summers." Wynne gave a rueful laugh. "The last summer—it was when I was twelve—he tolerated my tagging along. We tramped through the woods. He was working on a science project. He loved animals. A person like that doesn't commit murder."

"I wonder if you've gotten over that crush yet." Becca's voice was soft.

Wynne laughed. "Oh, no, I was just a kid."

"We'll see," Becca said. "Methinks the lady doth protest too much."

THREE

"I need you, Max," Simon pleaded. He hated to beg. "Steve gave me the names of other divers who might take his place, but no one could do it. I could dive alone, I guess." Everything in him cringed at the thought. He wasn't sure he was ready to go down.

"Absolutely not. You know that's not safe. There must be someone. You know I'd do it if I could." Max handed Simon a cup of coffee. "I've got several meetings on the mainland this week."

"I've got to have a diver." It was all Simon could do to sit still when everything in him cried out for action.

"Have you even been down since…?" He broke off his tentative question.

Simon hesitated, then shook his head. "Not yet."

Max gave him a kind look. "You need to climb back on that pony, Simon. It was a fluke. You've been a diver for years. Don't let one bad experience sap your joy."

Simon hunched his shoulders. "I know—I'll get

back down there. I have no choice now." The thought of putting on his gear and going under the waves again made him nearly gasp for breath. He didn't like to think of how he'd been trapped in a cave underwater for half an hour, how his oxygen was almost gone and spots had danced in front of his eyes like fish peering at him through his mask.

"Wynne could do it," Becca said from the doorway. She tugged Wynne into the room behind her.

Wynne was shaking her head even as Simon turned eagerly. "I've only got eight weeks until I have to be in Australia. I'd rather spend my time looking for an old ship. I'm sorry for your loss, Simon, but surely you can find someone else."

Simon looked at her. The red top she wore made her hair look even darker and more lustrous. His gaze fell to her bare feet. He had the feeling she would be comfortable in bare feet even at a fancy dinner.

He dragged his gaze back to her face. Something about those bare feet made him feel nostalgic and tender. He didn't care for the sensation. "I have to have someone. I'll pay you well."

She chewed on her lip. "I don't need the money."

He wanted to tell her she was being selfish, but bit back the words. "This is important. And you'd already agreed to be my cook."

"I thought you were joking, and that was when we were looking for something ancient anyway. Besides, your cousin's body has already been found. Why are you so keen to find the boat?"

"There has to be some reason for it to have gone down. There was no storm, no reason for it to sink."

"Faulty design?" she suggested. "I heard it was a prototype."

He jerked his head up. "I would have felt comfortable putting the president on that boat. It was a sound design. Innovative, yes, but safe."

"Yeah, like the *Titanic,* huh?"

He didn't dare answer her jibe or he knew he'd say more than he should and ruin all chance that she might help him.

"Wynne," Becca said in a reproachful voice.

A look of contrition crossed her face. "Sorry, Simon. You've just lost your cousin, and I think you're reacting to the stress of that. I just meant the *Titanic* incident proves you can never say a boat is safe. Things happen. You can't change this tragedy."

"I need to find out what happened to the boat."

"What happens when you find it? The sheriff will be looking, too."

"I can at least look around outside without bothering anything. We'll call Rooney and he can get someone inside to figure out what happened."

She pulled her long braid over her shoulder and sighed. "Okay, I'll help you. I'm sorry if I seemed unsympathetic. I'm not sure what you hope to discover, but I'll do what I can." A dimple appeared in her cheek. "I don't have to cook?"

He grinned. "I'm not averse to peanut butter sandwiches." He almost wanted to take back his plea for her help. Something inside shouted danger, though he couldn't see how this diminutive young woman could threaten him. Their shared history was a long time ago.

"It will be long, hard days," he warned.

Her smile faded, and red stained her cheeks. "You sound like you're trying to talk me out of it. Having second thoughts?"

He hadn't meant to offend her, but her composure bothered him. Something about her demeanor made him feel she was secretly laughing at him. But beggars couldn't be choosers, and in this instance, he needed her help. "You're hired," he said.

"I don't expect wages," she said. "But if you'll agree to help me search for older wrecks when this is all over, I'd be grateful."

"I'll pay you," he said. He felt out of control and didn't like the sensation. She didn't seem to care about who he was or how much he was worth. He reminded himself how he'd been wishing he could have a relationship like that.

Not that this was a relationship.

"What time should I meet you in the morning?" Wynne asked.

"Could you make it by seven?"

"It will be light by six." Her tone was almost a challenge.

"I'm an early riser. I'll see you at six."

He took his leave of Max and Becca and started toward town. The moon glimmered on Lake Superior as he walked along the shore drive. Craggy rocks and peaks loomed across the bay, their shadows reminding Simon of breaching whales or the Ojibwa thunderbird swooping low over the waves.

For a moment it seemed like an omen, then he shook off his fancies and turned toward home.

Wynne yawned as she sat on the balcony outside her bedroom and watched the sun come up. Her thick hair was still damp, but she braided it anyway, then wound it around the crown of her head and secured it with pins so it would stay out of her way.

She couldn't deny she was excited about what the day would bring. Watching Superior's waves crash against the rocks for the past few days had made her itch to be out on the water. Now she would get her chance. She didn't think they'd find anything out there, but much as she loved her family, she had chafed at the inactivity.

The *putt-putt* of a boat engine out on Superior drifted in her window, and she squinted at the white dot in the horizon as it made its way over the waves. Looked like the ferry. The sound brought back memories of riding the ferry every summer. She still could hardly believe she was here again.

The wind would likely be cool out on the Lake, so she pulled jeans and a long-sleeved cotton top over her modest swimsuit, then slid her feet into canvas mules. She met her sister with Isabelle in her arms on the verandah.

Becca's gaze roved over Wynne's face. "You look like you didn't sleep much last night."

Wynne grimaced. "Do I look that bad?"

"It would be impossible for you to look bad. You've just got shadows under your eyes. You nervous about going out with Simon?"

"No, I just had trouble sleeping." No way was she telling her sister the dream she'd had about Simon last night. Wynne took the baby and cuddled her. Isabelle put two fingers in her mouth and gave a contented sigh as she snuggled against Wynne's shoulder.

Becca looked at her watch. "I wonder where Max is. He's late."

"Is someone taking my name in vain?" Max asked, stepping through the sliding glass doors onto the verandah.

Becca kissed him. "I was just beginning to wonder where you were." She led him to the glass-topped table, already set with breakfast.

Wynne followed. She felt a little lonely watching them. She told her sister she didn't intend to get involved with a man, but seeing the love and closeness Becca and Max enjoyed made her realize how sterile her own life was.

Still, marriage would be a huge compromise, right? She'd have to give up adventure and new discovery for a relationship like theirs, and she didn't think she could do it. Though her brother Jake had managed.

He had sure stumbled into a sweet setup, and he was still engrossed in the dig on the other side of the island.

But when it was finished, would he be willing to settle down on the island and never crave a new thrill? Wynne didn't think so. Maybe she would stop over and see him and his bride that night when she got back.

She inhaled the sweet scent of baby powder. Maybe motherhood would be worth what she'd have to give up. She deposited Isabelle in her infant seat and slid into her chair. She'd likely never find out.

"It seems quiet with Gram gone." Their grandmother had gone on a trip with her best friend. She would be back in a few days.

Max nodded. "Going out with Simon today, right?"

"I guess."

Max raised his head at her tone. "You're going to like him when you get to know him. Just don't—" He broke off.

"Don't what?"

"Max," Becca said in a warning voice.

Wynne could hear the vibes. "What's going on?"

Becca gave a heavy sigh. She glanced at Wynne. "He was about to say keep it friends."

"You already told me." Surely she hadn't been sending out signals where Simon could get that notion.

"It's just—" Becca bit her lip and looked down.

"Just what?"

"We didn't talk about it enough earlier. I wanted you to be on your guard. All the women fall for Simon," Max said. "He's rich. Obscenely so. But that just makes him more wary of motives. We don't want to see you hurt. He's a great guy and all, but I doubt he'll ever let down his guard enough to fall for a woman."

"He fell for Amanda."

"I don't think he did, not really. I think he decided it was time to get married, and she seemed a likely candidate."

"That sounds a little cold." Wynne frowned and stabbed at a piece of melon. Simon hadn't struck her as the passionless type.

"Simon always considers things carefully. When he found out Becca was pregnant, I think it made him think of what he was missing." Max gave her a smile. "Just be on your guard. I don't want you hurt."

Wynne smiled. "Money doesn't impress me. And if you want the truth, Simon's type doesn't appeal to me at all. My heart is in no danger." Even as she said it, she knew she was kidding herself. His magnetism had grown stronger over the years.

After breakfast she walked down to the dock and waited. Simon should be along any minute. She heard the rumble of his boat mingled with the gentle sound of the surf. He waved, and she fluttered her fingers. Slinging her backpack over one shoulder, she went to the edge of the dock.

The white shorts he wore showed off strong, tanned legs, and his muscles flexed against his red shirt as he tossed her the rope to tie up. His dark hair gleamed in the sunlight. Her stomach felt funny. Maybe she was coming down with a bug because it surely couldn't be excitement over such a mundane search. When his hazel eyes met her gaze, she felt a shock of something she didn't want to name. The same something that had drawn her when she was a kid and he was a teenager.

Stupid. Even if she were interested—and she was not—he was way above her social status, as Max and Becca had pointed out. And the last thing she was going to do was make him think she was interested.

"Have trouble rolling out of bed?" she asked him.

"It's six-fifteen." He smiled. She'd never noticed he had a dimple in his chin.

"Holding me to a schedule? I thought I was the boss."

Her smile faltered. He was making sure she knew her place. Before she could construct a reply, she heard a shout behind her and turned to look.

A man she'd never seen jogged toward them. About thirty, he had a shock of brown hair that hugged his head in tight curls. He looked nice and ordinary.

"Brian, what are you doing here?" Simon called. He stepped from the boat to the dock.

Brian was out of breath when he reached them. "Glad I caught you. You can't leave yet. The sheriff is on his way."

Simon frowned. "Can't you handle it?"

The other man shook his head. "He said he needed to talk to you." His eyes widened when he saw Wynne, and he smiled. "Hello, I don't think we've met."

Wynne took the hand he extended. "Hi. Wynne Baxter."

"Jake and Becca's sister?"

She nodded. "Don't hold that against me." She pulled her hand from his grasp. The admiration in his glance warmed her, especially after Simon's caustic greeting.

"I've heard them talk about you. I'm Brian Lassiter, Simon's cousin." He stared at her.

Frowning, Simon cleared his throat. He shuffled from foot to foot and stared from Wynne to Brian and back to Wynne. What was his problem? Did he think his cousin was too good for her, too? She smiled up at Brian. Let Simon stew.

"You should stop by and see our boats sometime." Brian stepped to the *Thunderbird* and touched her hull. "This is just a sample of our work."

Wynne hadn't examined the boat before, so she followed Brian and looked over the lines of the craft. "She's beautiful. Did you design her?"

Brian nodded. "I'm the main designer. My brother also—" He stopped and looked down.

"I'm so sorry for your loss," Wynne said gently.

Brian looked up again. "Thanks. It's been a shock."

Wynne wondered what Simon did in the business. And why bother with all his money? "What's your job?" she asked him.

Brian answered for his cousin. "Simon takes care of the office. He counts the beans, or rather oversees the bean counters."

"Those beans could be better. This accident won't help," Simon said. He folded his arms across his chest.

Brian frowned and the open expression on his face closed.

Wynne could tell Brian didn't want to talk about the state of the business. She smiled uncertainly and tried to think of something else to say.

Gravel crunched beneath a vehicle's tires, and Wynne shaded her eyes with her hand. The sheriff had arrived. She watched Sheriff Rooney vault out of the car and hurry toward them.

"Glad I caught you," he huffed. "I need you to come down to the morgue."

Simon's restless movements stilled. "What's wrong?"

"We got another body." He gave Simon a glowering look. "It's Amanda."

"Amanda," Simon said slowly.

Rooney's gaze roamed over Simon's face. "Her parents are dead and her brother's on the mainland until tomorrow, so I guess you get elected as her next-of-kin for identification purposes. I need you to come down to the morgue."

By his tone, the sheriff seemed to be accusing Simon of something. His jaw was clenched, and he kept cracking his knuckles.

"Sure." Simon glanced at Wynne. "I'll call before I leave the morgue. I shouldn't be long."

"No problem." Wynne watched them walk away. The day seemed suddenly overcast, and she rubbed the gooseflesh on her arms. She didn't see how this new discovery could affect her, but she was convinced it was going to.

FOUR

Wynne's toes were frozen from their contact with the frigid water. Even in the summer, Lake Superior felt like melted snow. Gulls cawed overhead, and the sound of the surf soothed her, but the throb of a laboring motor soon drowned out the comforting noises.

She squinted against the sun in her eyes and stood. A boat limped toward the dock. The engine sounded like it was hitting on only two cylinders. The boat would be lucky to make it to the dock.

She raised her hand. "Ahoy. Do you need assistance?"

A man on the deck waved his hand over his head. The wind snatched his words away. Wynne hurried to the end of the dock and watched as the boat moved slowly toward her. When it came in range, the man tossed the rope to her. It fell into the lake, and she knelt to retrieve it from the cold water.

Tying it to the pier, she pulled on it to help guide the boat to the dock then wrapped the rope snug.

"Thanks." The man hopped ashore. Another man began to poke around at the motor while a woman about Wynne's age wrote in a log.

"I didn't think I was going to make it." The man was about forty with salt-and-pepper hair and shrewd blue eyes. His ruddy complexion had seen too much sun and wind. He held out his hand. "Mike Wilson."

She put her hand in his. "Wynne Baxter."

"Baxter. You must be the marine archaeologist I've heard about. I was thinking of calling you and seeing if you'd be interested in a summer job."

"You're on a marine archaeology dig?" Wynne was intrigued. She hadn't thought anyone was working in this area.

"Not exactly. I'm into ship salvage. Your expertise in locating sunken ships would help me find some wrecks. I need some help."

Wynne wrinkled her nose. "No thanks. No offense, but gutting our national treasures is the last thing I'd want to do." She expected him to get angry, but she didn't care.

He merely smiled. "I could make it worth your while."

"So you can sell the stuff to private investors?" She shook her head. "No thanks. I'd rather see my finds end up in museums where everyone can enjoy them."

"Well, if you change your mind, here's my card." He handed her a card that read Wilson Salvage.

"We've got it fixed, boss," the man at the engine called.

"I'd better get going," Wilson said. "Thanks for your time." He touched the bill of his ball cap then swung his long legs onto the deck of his boat.

Wynne wondered if they'd have future trouble with Mike Wilson. What if he found *Superior Lady* before they did? There was expensive technology on that yacht.

Simon shivered, not so much from the cold, sterile feel of the morgue, but from the dread that congealed in his stomach at what he was going to have to do. He followed Mitch Rooney down the colorless hall to the door at the end.

"In here." The sheriff held open the door. His stare held a trace of hostility.

Simon drew in a deep breath and forced himself to step into the room. Sweat broke out on his forehead in spite of the chill in the room. The coroner pulled back the sheet that covered the face of the figure on the table.

Simon sucked in his breath. "That's Amanda." He turned and bolted from the room, his stomach rebelling at the sight of the woman he'd thought to spend the rest of his life with. In the hallway, he leaned his forehead against the wall and tried to calm himself.

He sensed rather than heard the sheriff follow him. Swiping the back of his hand over his forehead, he turned to stare into the sheriff's face. He saw no sympathy in the man's expression.

"I'd like to ask you some questions," Rooney said.

"Fine." Simon squared his shoulders and followed him to a small room.

The sheriff stepped to a metal cart that held a coffee-pot and foam cups. "Coffee?"

"That'd be good." A shot of caffeine might strengthen him for what lay ahead. He could tell by the sheriff's manner that he was set to grill him.

The sheriff poured two cups of coffee and handed one to Simon. "Have a seat." He indicated two straight-backed chairs with worn seats in the corner.

Simon sat and took a sip of his coffee. The heat hit his stomach and began to thaw the ice running through his body.

The sheriff sat beside him. "When was the last time you saw your fiancée?"

"The day before she disappeared. Three months ago."

"Did you argue?"

Simon wished he didn't have to answer. "Yeah."

"Did she break off your engagement?" Rooney sounded hopeful.

"No." Simon perched his cup on his knee and stared into the dark liquid. He didn't dare tell the sheriff the specifics about their argument. The man would arrest him on the spot. "She said she'd see me in the morning."

"Where were you going to meet?"

"At the boat dock. We were going out for lunch. When I arrived, her car was there, but she wasn't. Jerry's car was there as well, but *Superior Lady* was gone. A fisherman on the dock told me she'd gone out with Jerry and she'd taken a suitcase."

"Did you try to find them?"

Simon nodded. "I tried to raise them on the radio, but Jerry never answered."

"You didn't go after them?"

"I tried but didn't find any sign of them."

"I'm sure you were angry."

"I spent three days looking for them until I realized they'd run off together." Simon shrugged. "It had happened before. Jerry always liked what someone else had."

"Kind of like you," Rooney sneered.

Simon had been trying to keep his cool, but Rooney's attitude was getting to him. Their history might get in the way of the investigation. He shot the sheriff a hard look. "Look, let's just get this out in the open. You don't like me. I understand that. But let's keep it to business, okay?"

Rooney's mouth tightened. "Fine," he said in a clipped tone. "Sounds like you disliked your cousin."

Simon blew out his breath. "Not at all. We were like brothers. I knew his faults just like he knew mine, but I loved him anyway." Simon swallowed as memories assailed him. Jerry laughing from the treehouse they'd built when Simon was ten; his excitement when they graduated from high school; the light in his eyes when he came up with the design for the *Superior Lady*. He'd been so sure blue skies were ahead and the three of them would be famous. Instead, he'd gone out on

Superior and had never come home. The futility of it all made Simon curl his fingers into his palms.

"Do you have any idea what could have happened to the boat—what caused it to sink?"

Simon shook his head. "It was innovative but safe. And the weather was perfect when they disappeared. That's why I was so certain Jerry had just gone off with Amanda. There was no reason for them to have had trouble out on the lake."

Sheriff Rooney stood and tossed his cup into the trash. "I'm sure I'll have more questions later so don't plan on taking any trips. Something smells fishy in all this, and I intend to get to the bottom of it."

"Has the coroner determined the cause of death for Jerry or Amanda?"

"Not yet. But he will."

The words sounded ominous the way he said them.

"I had nothing to do with their deaths." Simon knew his protestations of innocence wouldn't sway the sheriff, but he had to say them anyway. "Something must have gone wrong with the boat." As soon as the words were out of his mouth, he knew it was the wrong thing to say.

The sheriff's gaze sharpened. "Sabotage maybe?" he said, his voice deceptively soft.

"No, I mean a problem...." Simon's voice trailed away. The reality was there was no reason for the boat to have gone down. It was sound with a great engine they'd used on other boats.

"An engine explosion?"

"I don't see how," Simon admitted. "It had one of the best engines on it."

"Sabotage," the sheriff said again. "But you don't want to admit that. I wonder why?" His tone indicated he was already sure of the reason.

Simon drained his cup and tossed it into the trash. He wished he could get rid of the sheriff's suspicion as easily.

Wynne had plopped back on the dock, but her backside was starting to hurt from her hard seat. Glancing at her watch, she saw that Simon had been gone for an hour and a half. Surely he'd be back shortly. She should have gone back to Windigo Manor for a while, but the day was too beautiful to be spent inside. At least out there, she could feel the sun on her face and smell the scent of the lake.

She heard the sound of a vehicle and turned to see Simon get out of his truck. His eyes were shadowed, and his jaw looked as hard as Eagle Rock itself.

"Let's go," he said abruptly. He stalked to the boat and stepped onto the deck.

Wynne scrambled to her feet and hurried after him. With his mood obvious, she wouldn't put it past him to leave her if she lingered.

"Was—was it Amanda?" she asked quietly as he untied the rope and shoved the boat away from the dock.

"Yeah." Simon's jaw twitched.

A long silence descended as Simon fired the engine

and the bow lifted as the boat sped away from shore. Wynne wanted to ask more questions, but she could tell he was in no mood for chitchat.

"We'll stop and pick up the rest of the crew," Simon said. The boat moved toward the dock at Turtle Town.

A few minutes later, two men waved as the yacht pulled up to the dock. One was about forty with stringy blond hair pulled back at the nape of his neck. He wore ragged cutoffs and a black sleeveless T-shirt. The other was about thirty with a freckled nose and reddish hair. His interested gaze swept over Wynne as he stepped aboard *Thunderbird.*

"You're as pretty as I heard you were," he said. His snub nose was peeling from a sunburn.

"Cool it, Joe," Simon barked.

Wynne's smile faltered. Why did he sound so annoyed? She turned her smile back on full wattage. "I'm Wynne Baxter." She held out her hand.

"Joe Evans."

His firm grip enveloped her hand. He didn't seem to want to let go. She gently tugged her fingers free and turned her gaze to the man behind him.

"Hi." She held out her hand to the other man.

"Bjorn Poonen." He had a faint Scandinavian accent. He briefly touched her fingers, and his cool gaze slid by her. He nodded to Simon. "You're late, boss."

"Business to attend to. I should have called on your cell phone. Sorry." Simon revved the engine and the boat began to move away from the quay.

Wynne went to join Simon at the helm. "Where do you want to search first?" she asked as the shoreline disappeared. Gulls cawed over their heads, and the dull roar of the engine mingled with the sound of the wind and waves. The odor of oil and fuel drifted to her nose.

Simon whipped the wheel to the right and the boat veered. "Right about here," he said. "Jerry filed a trip itinerary in this direction."

"I would have thought you already looked here then," Wynne said.

"I did, but I didn't look under the water. I thought he might be out here floating around and enjoying himself. I never saw any trace of the *Superior Lady.*"

He moved to his equipment and began to fiddle with the controls. Joe slid into the seat at the panel. A beep began to sound as the sonar started to search below the surface of the water.

Joe stared at the screen. "Let's troll this meridian first." His finger jabbed at the screen.

"I can do that." She scrambled into the seat Simon had vacated. Watching her speed, she pressed the throttle and the boat began to move slowly through the water.

By three o'clock, they'd found nothing that showed up on the screen as more than rocks and boulders under the waves. Wynne knew they had a slim chance of finding *Superior Lady.* And it was going to be a long, hard time of it if Simon didn't speak. He'd sat beside her all afternoon and barely uttered a word.

The only sound had been that of the other two men talking in low tones out on the deck. She was tired of his attitude. What had she done?

She cut the engine, and his head jerked around. "Why are you stopping?"

"Look, if you want my help, you're going to have to talk to me. It makes too long a day to stare at the water and say nothing. I might as well be out here alone for all the company you've been."

His lips tightened. "It's not like we're best friends."

"True. But I'm not your enemy. We're on the same team. We might as well be friendly."

"I'm not good at small talk," Simon said as he stared back at the screen.

"I'm not talking about small talk. Tell me what you're seeing, talk about how you got interested in the Viking search and where you've looked. It will help pass the time."

"Maybe tomorrow."

"You want to talk about what happened at the morgue?"

Pain darkened his eyes. "The sheriff thinks I did it. I'm sure if we find the boat, we'll be ordered not to disturb it."

"Oh, surely not, Simon." Wynne couldn't imagine Simon in a rage. He'd been morose today, but not dangerous.

He shrugged. "I've been warned not to leave the island. Rooney is on a witch hunt, and I'm the one he has in mind for the stake."

"Why would he think that? Just because Amanda ran off with Jerry?"

"Pretty good motive, don't you think?"

"Did you suspect there was anything going on between them before they disappeared?"

He hesitated and looked away. "No."

She had a feeling he wasn't telling her the truth, and a feeling of disquiet swept over her. She pushed it away. Max considered Simon his best friend. He stoutly defended him. She was probably probing too hard.

"Why were you so sure then that Amanda was with Jerry?"

He shrugged. "Someone saw her board the boat with a suitcase."

"Do you have any idea where they were heading?"

He shook his head. "As far as I knew, Jerry was just going out for a few hours to test the *Superior Lady.* Amanda and I had planned to meet to discuss...things. When she was nowhere to be found, I asked around and discovered she'd gone off with Jerry."

He stated the words impassively. Wynne wondered how deeply he'd felt his fiancée's defection. "Let's see if we can figure out who might have wanted to harm either of them."

"Other than me, you mean?" His jaw tightened.

"Did Jerry have any enemies?"

"I've been wracking my brain about that all day."

"Explain to me the business setup. I don't want to be nosy, but where do you fit in?"

"I own about ten percent of the shipyard, but I don't take any money out yet. We're barely keeping our heads above water. Since I have an MBA, I run the office. Jerry was president, and Brian is vice president. Brian is the brains behind the designs while Jerry has always been the salesman. He could sell a refrigerator to an Eskimo."

"So with Jerry gone, how has business been going?"

Simon shrugged. "Okay, I guess. Brian and I have been trying to take up the slack. We figured Jerry would surface when he was good and ready."

Wynne was disliking Jerry more and more. "Did he have any enemies?"

Simon frowned. "We'd had to fire our manager two weeks before he disappeared. He'd embezzled ten thousand dollars. Right after that, we had a small fire in his old office. We managed to get it out before it did much damage, but I always wondered if he'd set it."

"Did the sheriff check it out?"

"That was in the days of Andrew Mitchell, and he couldn't be bothered. We never pressed charges about the embezzlement. Roger had been a friend of Jerry's for years, and Jerry didn't want to hurt Roger's wife, Teresa. She was an old girlfriend." He grinned. "Of course half the women in town were, too."

"Jerry must have been charming." And if he looked like Simon, it would have been a dangerous combination. Not that Simon wasn't appealing. His good humor and killer smile would have lured his own share of women.

"So this Roger could have wanted to get back at Jerry for being fired. And maybe he was jealous that Jerry had once dated Teresa."

"Maybe. Nothing adds up though. Killing Jerry wouldn't get Roger his job back. Look, we're barking up the wrong tree. I'm sure it was an accident."

He didn't sound sure. Wynne wondered why. "It might make him feel he'd evened the score. Is he still on the island?"

"Yeah. He opened a rival company. Shelby Boats."

Wynne had seen it the last time she'd gone to Turtle Town. "Even more of a reason," she pointed out. "If the *Superior Lady* was such an innovation, maybe he was afraid of being run out of business."

"He hadn't opened it yet." Simon stretched his long legs along the deck.

He was so overwhelmingly male. His strong legs were tanned and muscular. Wynne turned her gaze away. "Have you seen his boats? Could he be using the design of the *Superior Lady?*"

"That would be stupid. I'd recognize it right off. He hasn't launched anything yet."

"Any possibility of our getting a look in his shop?"

"He'd never let me in there."

Wynne bit her lip. There had to be a way. "Max has been thinking of buying a new boat. Maybe I could get him to call, and me and Max could go look."

"Roger would likely be suspicious. He knows me and Max are friends, and I would likely be Max's choice of a builder."

"True, but what can he say if Max calls? It's worth a try."

Simon looked up, and his gaze was intent. "Why are you doing this? It isn't your problem. I hired you to help find the boat, not solve a murder."

Murder. It was an ugly word, and it was the first time anyone had spoken it, though she'd thought it. "You think it was murder, don't you?"

Simon was silent for a long moment. "I don't see how that boat could have gone down," he said. "So maybe I do. I hope I'm wrong."

"I hope so, too," she said. More than he knew. If the sheriff deemed it homicide, they had their work cut out for them to prove Simon's innocence.

FIVE

"Brian, you in here?" Simon walked through the boat plant, his shoes squeaking on the concrete floor. The place had that deserted feel, but he'd seen Brian's car out back. He dreaded telling Brian the news.

"Is he here?" Wynne whispered.

"He has to be here somewhere. His car is outside."

"Maybe he left with someone else."

A noise came from their left, then Brian's head appeared over the top of the bulkhead.

He stopped when he saw them. He began to smile when he saw Wynne. "You looking for me? I was working on the brightwork." He joined them. Brian's smile faltered when he saw the expression on Simon's face. "I'm sorry, Simon. I know it must be hard."

"Thanks." Simon hadn't had time to examine how he felt. When Amanda left him, he'd been hurt but had soon realized he'd just been lonely, and she filled the spot. He'd thought she really loved him. For the first time, he began to wonder if she'd left with Jerry for another reason. He gave a slight shake of his head. She had her suitcase with her. He was grasping at straws.

He dragged his attention back to his cousin. "Thanks. What else did the sheriff say?"

"He—he asked a lot of questions."

"About me?"

Brian nodded. "He wanted to know what you and Amanda had argued about the day before she disappeared with Jerry."

Luckily, Brian didn't know what the argument was about. Simon gave a nod. "What else?"

"Whether there were any disagreements between you and Jerry."

"He didn't ask about any other enemies Jerry might have had?"

"No."

"He thinks he's found his man, and I'm it." Simon's gaze met Wynne's, and the sympathy in her eyes lifted the cloud he'd been fighting all day. She didn't really know him, yet she believed him. The more he was around her, the more he appreciated what he saw. She would be a powerful ally to anyone.

The front door banged, and Simon heard an angry shout.

"Lassiter, I know you're in here!"

It sounded like Amanda's brother, Alan Whistler. Simon turned to see Alan stalk between two boats. His too-small head looked incongruous with his linebacker body. Dark eyes set too close together completed a picture of a body that didn't quite go together.

"Hello, Alan." Simon stepped out to intercept him.

Alan didn't answer. He came at Simon with both fists swinging. Simon ducked and caught Alan's right wrist in his hand. Stepping into the punch, Simon flipped Alan around with his arm behind his back.

"Let me go!" Alan struggled to get free.

Simon caught a whiff of alcohol. "Calm down and I will."

Alan began to weep, a *huh-huh-huh* sound that sounded like it was ripping his throat apart. He dropped to his knees and covered his face with his hands. Simon curled his fingers into his palm. He wanted to comfort Alan, but the two had never been the best of friends.

Wynne glanced at Simon with confusion on her face. *Who is he?* she mouthed.

Amanda's brother, he mouthed back. She nodded. The comprehension flooding her face was followed with sympathy.

She knelt beside Alan and put her arm around his shoulders. "I'm sorry about your sister," she said. "We're trying to find the boat to see if we can discover what happened."

Alan raised his head. "I know what happened," he said, his voice choked. He raised his hand and pointed at Simon. "He murdered Amanda and Jerry."

Wynne's hand dropped. She stood and backed away from Alan. "Your grief is clouding your judgment."

He looked at Wynne. "Who are you anyway? His new girlfriend? His money isn't worth it." He spat the words and stood, ramming his hands into the pockets of his jeans.

Simon clenched his fists. "That's enough, Alan," he said. "I know you're upset, but you don't need to take it out on Wynne. This is Wynne Baxter."

Alan's scowl faded. "Baxter? You're related to the Baxters of Windigo Manor?"

"She's Becca's sister," Brian put in.

Alan sneered at Simon. "Going for respectability? Even hooking up with a Baxter won't wash away what you are."

Simon rubbed his head. "Look, go home, Alan. You're not making sense. I know you're upset, and I'm sorry about that. But bandying words with me isn't going to change things. I'm going to do all I can to find out what happened to *Superior Lady.*"

"Yeah, right." Alan stomped toward the door then turned. "Any spin you put on it will cover up what really happened." He looked at Wynne. "Ask him what he and Amanda fought about the day before she disappeared."

Simon could feel Wynne's eyes on him, could sense the question in her eyes. "Go home, Alan," he repeated wearily. He wasn't up to discussing this anymore today. He tried to roll with the punches, but they kept coming, and he felt battered.

Alan gave him a final glare and stomped from the boathouse. Moments later the roar of his vehicle came through the open door.

Brian looked at him. "What was the argument about? You've never said."

"And I'm not going to now," Simon said. He took Wynne's elbow. "Let's go."

The verandah overlooked Superior's blue water. A cedar waxwing warbled from a branch over Wynne's head. She dug out her bird journal and jotted it down. She tossed some toast crumbs to the flagstone floor, and the songbird flew down to peck at the morsels.

"Still bird-watching?" Becca joined her at the table.

"So far, I've added four new birds—a yellow-rumped warbler, a rough-legged hawk, a cedar waxwing and a Harris' sparrow."

"You're hopeless." Becca handed Wynne the baby.

Wynne nestled little Isabelle against her shoulder, and the baby put her thumb in her mouth and closed her eyes. Gazing at the rosebud mouth, Wynne felt a surge of motherly instinct. She laid her lips on Isabelle's soft head and breathed in the aroma of baby. The more she was around her niece, the more she envied her sister.

Becca flipped idly through Wynne's bird diary. "What time are you supposed to meet Simon?"

"About ten. He had some things to do this morning." She chewed on a ragged thumbnail. Maybe she should back away from working with Simon.

Becca's head came up. "Is that reserve I hear in your voice? Did things not go well yesterday? We didn't get a chance to talk last night."

"Things went fine other than Simon is under suspicion for murdering his cousin and his fiancée."

Becca winced. "Serious suspicion? I don't believe it. Simon is a great guy."

"Even great guys get caught up in passion." Wynne hadn't wanted to entertain any suspicions about Simon, but it was hard to stay objective with the mounting accusations. "I don't want it to be true, but it's hard when he acts guilty."

"How does he act guilty?"

Wynne told her sister how Simon refused to talk about the argument he'd had with Amanda.

"But that could just be because it was painful," Becca offered.

"Yeah, but you have to admit it looks suspicious."

Before Becca could answer, a deep voice carried through the open French doors. "Where're those baby sisters?"

"We're out here, Jake," Becca called.

Wynne's tension melted away as her brother and his wife joined them on the verandah. She'd hardly seen them so far this trip. Skye's round stomach suited her. Her black hair was tied back in a ribbon, and her smile was full of contentment.

"Skye, you look ready to pop," Wynne said. She pushed a spare chair out with her foot. "Sit down."

"I feel great." Skye ran her hand over Isabelle's fuzzy head. "Does she sleep all the time?"

"She's starting to stay awake more." Becca's smile was indulgent.

"I can't wait," Skye said, running her hand over her protruding belly.

"How about you, big brother? You ready to be a dad?" Wynne teased.

"About as ready as a chicken is to take wing," Jake said. "I'm scared spitless." He touched the baby with a finger. "I was fine until this little morsel was born and I saw how tiny a newborn really is. I'm afraid I might break her."

"Don't be silly." Becca lifted her daughter from Wynne's arms and handed her to Jake, whose expression was a mixture of terror and elation. The baby opened her eyes and looked at her uncle, then promptly went back to sleep.

"You're losing your touch," Wynne said. "Women used to be wide-awake around you and your charm."

"It's all Skye's fault. She's ruined me for any other woman." Jake cradled the baby's head in his big hands.

"I have a feeling our new son will upstage me," Skye said.

"It's a boy?" Wynne and Becca said at the same time.

Jake and Skye burst into laughter. "If you could see the expression on your faces," Skye said. "I had an ultrasound yesterday. It's a boy!"

"A nephew," Wynne said. She should be elated, but a hollow feeling settled into her stomach and refused to go away. Soon her brother and sister would be caught up in their own lives. She'd be just a peripheral figure. While she was happy for them, she knew loneliness was going to become a constant companion.

"Why aren't you out scouring the deep for a Viking ship?" Jake's eyes were mocking.

Wynne made a face at him. "I know it sounds crazy. But we're not really looking for the Vikings now. We're searching for the *Superior Lady* that went down about three months ago."

"Not quite your style."

"Haven't you heard about the bodies that surfaced?" Wynne asked.

"I haven't listened to the news today," her brother said. He handed Isabelle to her mother when she started to fuss. "What's up?"

Wynne told him about the murder accusations. "So you see we need to find that boat."

"I'm not sure I like you getting involved in this," Jake said. "I'm not suspicious of Simon, but if this really is murder, whoever did it is not going to like you poking around. He or she might decide to come after you."

"You think it could be a woman?" Wynne was intrigued with the idea. Most murders were committed by men, and she'd just assumed it was a man.

"You never know. Did Jerry have a girlfriend?"

"He'd had lots of them, from what I understand. Did you ever meet him?" Wynne decided she'd pump her brother while he was in a talkative mood.

"Once. I ran into him with Simon in Turtle Town, and Simon introduced us. I can't say I was impressed with him. He kept boasting about how his boats were the best out there. And he paid too much attention to Skye."

Skye laughed. "That's his real objection. I liked Jerry."

Jake gave his wife a doting look. "I didn't like it, that's all. Some jealous girlfriend or husband could have decided he'd gone too far."

"Simon fits that category, too," Wynne pointed out. She stood and stretched. "I'd better get to the dock."

"Talk to you later," her siblings called.

She walked down the hillside to the dock. An Ojibwa fisherman was putting away his gear when she arrived.

He gave her a long, slow look from under his bushy brows. "You're the woman who disturbs the boats," he said.

"I search for shipwrecks," she corrected. She didn't know whether to be alarmed or not. He seemed harmless.

"It's not wise to disturb the dead," he said. "The *Thunderbird* will punish us all." He stepped closer, and she took a step back. "You should leave this island. There is nothing for you here."

"I have a job to do," she said.

"You can't do anything if you're dead," he said, taking up his fishing pole and bait box.

He left her standing there with her mouth agape.

SIX

Wynne glanced at Simon from the corner of her eye as he grappled with the anchor. The wind had freshened today, rocking the boat. It was going to be hard to keep it in the same area. The lake was deep here, deeper than their anchor could reach. They'd have to troll back and forth in the area to stay put.

Joe tapped the sonar screen. "Something looks interesting down there," he said, jabbing his finger at a mass on the screen. "What do you think?"

"It might be something," Simon conceded. He glanced at Wynne. "Want to go down and have a look?"

"I'm in the mood to dive." Wynne pulled her dry suit up and thrust her arms into the fabric. The unknown beckoned, and she was eager to get below the waves and explore.

"I got our rebreathers ready. The floor is about a hundred and fifty feet down. You game to go that deep?" His voice was low and he didn't look at her.

"Absolutely." Deep diving was her favorite, as there were fish and marine life that people rarely saw otherwise. He helped her into her rebreather, and she held his out for him to slip his arms into.

Bjorn tossed the anchor overboard. Wynne looked at Simon. "You look a little pale. You okay?"

"The boss man does look a little green around the gills," Joe said.

"I'm fine," Simon barked.

Wynne raised her brows at his tone. "What's eating you?"

He pressed his lips together. "Ready to go down?"

He wasn't going to tell her anything. She wondered if the sheriff had been harassing him again. She shrugged and adjusted her mask. Simon stepped aside for her to reach the rail. She perched on the side of the boat then fell backward into the water.

Wynne breathed steadily through her mouthpiece. The silence of the rebreather, as opposed to a regulator and tank, always enthralled her. She could focus on what her eyes saw instead of being distracted by the sound of the bubbles.

She glanced around, but still didn't see Simon. Peering up through the water, she saw him staring down at her from the boat. What was his problem?

She kicked her fins and shot to the top. "Are you coming in?"

Perspiration beaded his forehead. "I'm coming. Give me a minute."

His knuckles were white where he gripped the side

of the boat. She glanced at Bjorn and saw sympathy on his normally stoic face.

He saw her gaze and shrugged. "He will not tell you, but he almost drowned the last time he went down at the end of last summer. He has not been down since."

Wynne went to the ladder. "You don't have to come down with me. Bjorn, can you join me instead?"

The blond man shook his head. "Neither of us are trained in deep dives."

"Hey." Simon waved his hand. "I'm still here, guys. I'm not some ghost." He managed a feeble grin. "I'll be fine. Just give me a minute."

Wynne had never experienced fear of the water, but with her fear of snakes she could identify with the fear and tension that took hold of Simon's body. "I'll hold your hand while we go down."

Simon's sickly grin widened. "I might take you up on it."

"I sure would, boss," Joe said, leering at Wynne.

She laughed and held out her gloved hand. "You can do it, Simon."

"I have a feeling you were a cheerleader in school." He adjusted his mouthpiece and went over the side with a splash.

She gave Simon the thumbs-up and held out her hand. He gripped it, and they began the descent. Simon swam slowly beside her. She glanced into his eyes and saw interest and intent begin to push aside fear. He was going to be okay.

A school of lake herring, a shimmer of pink and

purple iridescence, darted past, and she paused to enjoy the sight. They'd once been in decline, but were now coming back in the western part of the lake.

Simon pointed, and she paused to gawk at the largest muskie she'd ever seen. The silvery-green fish was over five feet long. They let it swim by, then continued to head down to the lake bottom. They paused often to let their ears equalize to the pressure. As they neared the bottom, Wynne reached out and clutched Simon's arm. She pointed to a ship resting on the bottom.

It wasn't a yacht, but it was a perfectly preserved steamer from the 1800s. From its condition, she was sure no one else had found it. Looking for a name on its hull, she swam around it and startled a school of whitefish. They flashed past her in a blur of movement. She flailed back out of their way and bumped into Simon.

She could see his grin through his mask. He pointed at the hull, and she made out the ship's name—*Windigo Wind.* Running her hand along the letters, Wynne wondered how long it had been since human eyes looked at the boat. How many had gone down with this ship and what had caused it to sink? In her mind's eyes, she saw storms lash the side and heard men shouting out orders.

She gave herself a mental shake. This wasn't the boat she'd come down here to find. The powerful beam of her halogen light touched the hull. She itched to be able to investigate this ship. Their first dive, and they'd hit the jackpot.

Reluctantly, she left it behind and swept the beam of her light beyond the sunken ship. Rock formations loomed out of the shadows, but nothing was the right size or shape to be the *Superior Lady.*

A boat passed by overhead, and she glanced at her watch, realizing more time had passed than she'd realized. They'd been investigating for nearly an hour. Simon pointed upward, and she nodded. This wasn't the site they sought. They ascended slowly, pausing at the proper levels to allow their bodies to decompress.

Wynne was still exhilarated by the time she climbed aboard the boat. "What a find," she exclaimed as she tugged off her flippers. "When we've found the *Superior Lady,* I'd like to go back down there and investigate it some more."

Simon seemed to be paying no attention. He muttered something under his breath and moved quickly toward two figures on the deck.

Wynne gasped. Joe and Bjorn were lying unconscious on the deck. Blood pooled under Bjorn's head, and an ugly bruise marred Joe's forehead and cheek. She rushed to help Simon tend to them.

Joe groaned as she touched him. Wynne helped him sit up. "What happened?" she asked.

He put his head in his hands. "Someone dressed in a black dry suit clobbered me. I'd noticed a boat anchored about two hundred yards away, but hadn't paid any attention. The diver must have swum from the boat. I heard a noise and turned to see Bjorn already down and some yahoo coming at me with a tire iron."

Simon had Bjorn sitting up as well. "We need to get you both to the hospital."

"I'll be okay." Joe staggered to his feet, and Wynne pulled a chair forward for him.

Bjorn just leaned against the bridge. "I think I will sit here for now," he muttered.

"Call the Coast Guard," Wynne told Simon.

"Look at the equipment." He pointed to the controls. She inhaled at the sight of the smashed dials.

"Someone doesn't want us to find the boat," he said.

"Maybe. We'd better let the sheriff decide what went on here." She didn't want to jump to conclusions. "Maybe it has to do with the boat we found. The *Windigo Wind*."

His cheeks turned a dull red. "I tend to jump to conclusions. I forgot about the steamer. So much for being James Bond." He grinned.

"You've got the looks for it," she quipped as he started the engine. She put her hand over her mouth and wished she could call back the words.

"Ah, you've noticed," he said, his smile widening. "Here I thought you were immune to the Lassiter charm."

"So you're a good-looking guy," she said nonchalantly. "I see handsome men all the time. It's what's inside that counts."

"And I'm failing in that regard?"

"I'm reserving judgment," she said.

Water gleamed on his tanned face. She could see he was trying to squelch his grin. For the first time, she wondered if she'd bitten off more than she could chew by agreeing to help him. She wasn't in the market for a broken heart, but she could hear the lyrics of "Heartbreak Hotel" in her head. She was going to have to be on her guard after all.

Wynne's gaze caught on something on the floor. "What's this?" She knelt and picked up the shiny piece of metal gleaming in the sunshine.

"Let me see." Simon took it from her hand and flipped it over. "Looks like a charm. It's not yours?"

"I never wear jewelry. It gets in the way." The charm was in the shape of a bird. "Is it supposed to be a thunderbird?"

"Looks like it, yeah." He held it out to show the other two men. "You guys ever see this?"

"Nope," Joe said. His color was returning.

"Me neither," Bjorn said. "It's not mine."

Wynne glanced at the smashed equipment and the blood on the deck. "Could it be a warning?"

Simon frowned. "A warning? How?" He followed her gaze then grinned. "You mean you think the thunderbird doesn't like us being out here?"

"Maybe. It sounds fantastic, doesn't it?" She laughed. "Next thing you know I'll be hiring a medicine woman to protect us. But a fisherman on the dock warned me to let the dead lie. He said the *Thunderbird* wouldn't like it if I disturbed the shipwrecks."

"As long as you don't go bringing chicken bones onboard, we're okay."

Though he'd joked with her, Simon wondered if he should make her stay home. It could have been Wynne lying on the deck. If someone hit a tiny thing like her with a tire iron, she wouldn't walk away from it like Joe and Bjorn.

His crew had been treated and released at the hospital. The sheriff had been called, but it was clear he thought they were trying to pull something to get him off the scent.

The charm was in his pocket, and he fingered it as he drove toward the boatyard. He should track down the fisherman and talk to him, though it seemed a stretch to think anyone would believe the old legends enough to try to scare them into abandoning their search. But maybe the murderer had put the man up to it.

He stopped at his own thoughts. The murderer. Did he really believe someone had killed Jerry and Amanda? No, he decided. The most likely scenario was still a malfunction in the boat. He had to find the yacht just to set his own mind at ease.

He went in search of Brian as soon as he reached the boatyard. He found his cousin working on his chess set. He'd been carving it for three years now, and with each piece, Simon marveled at the patience Brian showed for the intricate detail. It was the same care he took with his yacht creations.

"Hey," Brian said, glancing up from his work. He set aside a king chess piece. "How'd it go today?"

"We found an old steamer but no sign of our boat." Simon propped his boot on a log. "Have you seen an old Ojibwa fisherman around?" He described the man Wynne had seen.

"Sounds like it might be Old Robert."

"Old Robert?"

"He's an old Ojibwa medicine man. His mission is to make sure the old ways aren't forgotten."

"Any idea where I can find him?"

"Check Bob's Eats. He hangs out there when he's not fishing."

Simon thanked his cousin and jogged back to his truck. It was probably nothing, but he wanted to set his mind at rest.

SEVEN

Wynne held her breath as the yellow American goldfinch edged closer to the morsel of bread she held in her hand. She hadn't moved in five minutes, and her muscles screamed from the effort of keeping so still. The bird finally grabbed a crumb and flew up to the limb above her head. She stood and released her muscles from their torment.

All around her, the forest was alive with sound: the gurgle of the brook that ran merrily to Lake Superior, the warble of the birds, wind soughing through the evergreens and the stand of white birch.

"Looking for the thunderbird?"

She turned at the sound of her brother's voice. "Jake, you about scared me to death. I thought no one else was out here. How did you know where to find me?"

"Becca told me you'd be out birding. I thought you would have outgrown that hobby by now."

"Never." She tossed the last of the crumbs to the ground and watched as a flock of sparrows fluttered down to plunder the remains. She dusted her hands on her jeans. "Is anything wrong?"

"Becca called me about the attack."

Wynne rolled her eyes. "You'd think she was the oldest instead of the youngest. Motherhood has changed her."

"I don't want you in any danger, Wynne. Maybe you'd be better off to let Simon fight his own battles."

"I'll be fine. The men will be on their guard from now on." She tried to inject confidence into her voice, but it fell flat.

"Yeah, and I love onions," he said, rolling his eyes.

"You worry too much."

"And you never look at reality." He guided her toward the path out of the woods. "It's almost dinner-time. You're probably starved."

"I always am after a dive. But I filched a peanut butter sandwich before I came out here."

"Looks like you fed most of it to the birds."

Wynne stopped. "Do you think Simon did it?"

"I thought he was underwater with you."

"Not the attack. I mean, do you think he sank that boat?"

"I don't know him all that well." Her brother eyed her. "If you think there's even a remote possibility he could be guilty, you need to back away from this."

"Why would he be so determined to find the boat if he did it?" No matter how hard she tried to imagine

Simon as a murderer, she kept coming back to that fact. "Unless he's not really looking. Maybe he knows where it went down and is deliberately keeping us from going in that direction. It would keep the sheriff off his back if Simon makes what seems to be a sincere effort to find the boat."

Jake had stopped on the path, and his frown deepened as she spoke. "I don't like this, Wynne. Do you have any reason to suspect he's leading you on a wild-goose chase?"

She didn't know why she was talking this way. The last thing she wanted to believe was that Simon was a cold-hearted murderer. To spend her days with him she had to trust him. And she couldn't just walk away from the opportunity to plunge into the cold water and see what she might discover in the lake's depths, not without some kind of evidence.

"You've got that look on your face," Jake observed.

"What look?"

"The one that says you're trying to convince yourself of something. You get a little vertical line between your eyes, and you scrunch your nose up like this."

Wynne laughed at her brother's imitation of her. "I do not."

"You do. I think you want to keep the handsome Simon at arm's length, and thinking he could do something sinister is a way to do just that."

"That's ridiculous," she said. She turned and stalked toward the house. "Just because you're playing house now doesn't mean you have to foist your version of happiness on every single person."

"You're not every single person. You're my sister. I want you to be happy."

Jake sounded amused and she wanted to hurt him. "I am perfectly happy with my life." She strode along the pine-strewn path ahead of him. Her words sounded hollow, even to herself.

Jake fell into step beside her. "What kind of life is it to be traipsing all over the world with no real place to call home?"

"It's the same life you had for years," she pointed out.

"Yeah, but I had no idea how much better hearth and home were."

"You sound positively evangelistic about it." The corners of her mouth twitched and she clamped her lips together. She would not laugh. It would just encourage him.

He caught her by the arm and stopped her headlong plunge toward the house. "If I am it's because I sense you're a little lost right now, Wynne. I want you to be happy, but I don't want to see you grab the first available man who happens by. And you haven't been worshiping much lately, have you? I can always tell."

She decided to ignore his comment about worship. She would fix that soon." If I were stupid enough to grab the first available man, I would already be married."

"True." Jake sounded resigned. "Gram is home now. She's wondering where you are."

Wynne began again toward the house. "I'm eager to see her!"

* * *

Bob's Eats bustled with residents of Turtle Town. Though as the only place to eat in town, it could have gotten away with poor food, the choices were surprisingly tasty and the coffee hot and fresh. Simon pushed past a group of men who stank of fish and scanned the room. He didn't really know who he was looking for. Many of the men in the dining room were Ojibwa.

He stopped the waitress, Rhonda. "Hi, Rhonda, do you—"

She interrupted before he could ask her. "I heard about Jerry." Her eyes were red.

He'd forgotten she'd dated his cousins—first Brian, then Jerry. "Yeah, it's a shock." He pressed her arm. "Hey, do you know Old Robert? Is he here?"

She pushed a strand of hair out of her eyes that had escaped the band at her neck and pointed to a man sitting alone at a table in the corner. "There."

"Thanks." Simon wove through the tables and stopped in front of the table. "Robert?"

Dressed in a red plaid shirt and jeans with suspenders, Old Robert's eyes had dark bags, and he sported a two-day's growth of beard. He took a sip of his coffee then pushed the other chair out with a booted foot. "Sit."

Simon pulled the chair out farther then sat down. "Did you talk to Wynne Baxter this morning?"

The old Native American man took his time about answering. "I talk to everyone at the dock. She the pretty gal with dark curly hair?"

"That's her. You told her to leave the boat where it lies. You indicated she might be in danger if she disturbed it. Do you have any information about where it is, or who sank it?" He'd finally said it—admitted someone had to have sunk the boat. Was that easier to believe than that the design was flawed?

Old Robert shook his head. "I've seen the signs. The thunderbird is angry and wants the water graves to be undisturbed. Poking around old wrecks is wrong. Let the dead rest."

Simon leaned forward. "You are on the water all the time. Have you seen anything that might indicate the boat was sunk on purpose?"

"I see many things. Some things are better left alone." The old man stood and dropped several bills onto the table.

Old Robert knew something. Simon stood, too. "Please. Tell me what you know. I have to know the truth."

"No good can come from stirring up a hornet's nest. Go home. Forget about the yacht. Your cousin and your friend are dead. Nothing can bring them back. Revenge isn't worth the price."

"I don't want revenge, I just want to know what happened. Besides, the sheriff thinks I did it."

"There will be no proof of anything if the boat is never found. Leave it alone." Old Robert turned and walked toward the door.

Simon didn't try to stop him. The old man wasn't giving up any information. If he even knew anything.

Maybe he just liked to act like a wise man and issue portents and ominous warnings.

"Want to order something?" Rhonda stood at the table with her pen and pad in her hand. Simon's stomach rumbled. "I take that as a yes," she said with a laugh.

"I guess I am hungry." Simon smiled and grabbed the menu. "Bring me a beef pasty and some fries. Coffee, too."

"You got it. Old Robert have any information?"

"Not really."

"I figured as much. He likes to act important. I wouldn't take anything he said as gospel." She tucked the pen into the pocket of her apron and went to the kitchen.

Simon's head had begun to ache. He was never going to figure this out. Lake Superior was vast. It was a long shot to even look for the yacht. Maybe Old Robert was right and he should leave it to the sheriff. The lawman had no proof Simon had done anything, and he wasn't likely to find any. A deep voice interrupted Simon's thoughts.

"Mind if I join you?" The sheriff didn't wait for an answer to sit in the seat Old Robert had vacated.

"It's a free country." He wasn't in the mood to be grilled anymore today.

"Finding anything?" the sheriff asked.

All the doubts about continuing to look vanished at the other man's skepticism. "It's early days yet. I'll find *Superior Lady.*"

"I did a little poking around today, Lassiter. Your cousin was the kind of guy who stepped on a lot of toes. Quite the womanizer. Did you just get tired of it finally? Why not get it off your chest and tell me all about it?"

"Any results back on the autopsies?" Simon asked.

"Not yet. What do you think I'll find?"

Simon rose and threw his napkin on the table. "You can have my dinner, Sheriff. I find my appetite is gone." He rushed past the waitress and hurried out the door. The sheriff might not have any real evidence yet, but if he figured out the fight, would that be enough to bring changes against him?

EIGHT

Wynne swung lazily on the porch and watched the stars come out. She saw a sweep of headlights, then an unfamiliar truck stopped. She recognized Simon as he got out. The surge of excitement that swept through her took her aback. Maybe Jake knew her better than she knew herself.

Simon smiled when he saw her. "I just stopped by to tell you I found Old Robert."

"Old Robert?"

"The Ojibwa fisherman you talked to. I think he knows something, but he's not telling."

"You talked to him? What if you made him mad and he comes looking for me because I blabbed?" Wynne wouldn't want to face the old fisherman on a dark night. She shivered.

Simon took her hand and squeezed it. "I don't think he's dangerous."

It was hard to think with his strong fingers holding hers. "Someone on this island is."

"I want to believe the boat was faulty."

Wynne's words dried on her tongue as they stared at one another a moment. "But you don't think so, not really."

"We've got to find that yacht."

"We can hit it fresh tomorrow." Her earlier doubts swept away. She could trust this man. The crunch of gravel caught her attention, and she turned to see a big luxury car stopping in front of the manor.

A short, heavyset man dressed in neatly pressed slacks got out. The scowl on his face deepened when he saw them. "I thought that was your truck, Lassiter," he growled.

Feeling Simon's tension, Wynne glanced up into his face. His grip on her fingers had tightened to a painful squeeze.

"Roger, what are you doing here?" he said through tight lips.

Roger. Wasn't that the name of the manager who had been fired just before the boat went down? Wynne's curiosity kicked into gear. She gave a tentative smile, but the angry man didn't notice. He continued to glare at Simon.

"I've been looking for you. You sicced the law on me. I told the sheriff you were just trying to throw suspicion off yourself." Roger smiled grimly. "I think he believed me."

"I didn't tell the sheriff anything about you." Simon's tone was cool.

Roger gave a snort. "Yeah, and I believe that about

as quick as I'd believe I could drive this car across Lake Superior. You've had it in for me since day one, haven't you?"

"I didn't make you embezzle the money, Roger."

Roger winced. "I was going to pay it back!"

"How?"

Roger just scowled. "My business is doing just fine. If you'd just been patient, I could have paid you back."

Simon pushed on relentlessly. "You still can. Did you hope the fire would kill Jerry? When it didn't, maybe you decided a boat accident would be a safer choice."

Roger was shaking his head before Simon finished talking. Wynne didn't know what to think. Roger seemed full of anger, but it was more a righteous indignation at the thought that someone suspected him of murder.

"I should have known better than to try to talk to you," Roger said bitterly. He got in his car and slammed the door. The engine roared to life, and gravel kicked from under the tires as he sped away.

Wynne felt shaken though it wasn't even her problem. She suddenly realized she had Simon's fingers in a death grip. She'd held onto him through the entire confrontation.

He didn't seem to mind.

Returning the pressure of his fingers, she smiled up at him. "I feel like we just lived through a waterspout."

"And that describes Roger. He's all blow." Simon stood looking down into her eyes.

A shiver started at the base of her neck and worked its way down her spine as she looked into his eyes. She told herself it was just a reaction to seeing her brother and sister so happy, but deep down she knew Simon had always intrigued her.

She swallowed. "I smell tonight's meat loaf. The least I can do is make sure you get fed tonight. Come with me." She tugged at his hand then finally released it when they reached the front door.

"You don't need to do that." His protest was weak.

He followed her inside where Max and the rest of the family greeted him. Gram rose and went to him, and he kissed her cheek. "You finally decided to come home?"

"Did you miss me?" Her bright blue eyes twinkled as she looked at him.

"Always." She took his arm, and he led her toward the dining room.

Wynne tailed behind, ashamed to notice her nose was out of joint at the way Gram hijacked Simon. But what did she expect? Him to suddenly find her overwhelmingly attractive? What a laugh. Wynne could just imagine what Amanda had been like—probably a blonde with perfectly coiffed hair, expertly applied makeup, clothing that shouted Saks and diction that betrayed her education at an Ivy League school.

He wouldn't be interested in a bohemian type like her. She didn't wear shoes half the time. And her education had come from a plain-Jane variety Midwestern college. The way she'd found a job in her field had more to do with her tenacity and passion than her education.

Besides, she wasn't interested in him, so why was she piqued at his lack of interest?

Wynne resolved to catch up with Becca and forget what the handsome Simon was up to. She moved beside her sister. Isabelle began to fuss.

"I'll take her," Gram said. "I'm not hungry anyway. You young ones get started, and I'll join you as soon as I get the baby settled down."

Before Wynne realized what was happening, she found herself herded by Becca toward the seat Gram had vacated next to Simon. Becca had a self-satisfied look on her face as she grabbed the back of the chair across the table from Wynne and pulled it out. Wynne crossed her eyes at her sister, and Becca gave a smothered giggle.

"Something wrong?"

Wynne's face went hot as she looked up into Simon's quizzical face. "Not at all," she stammered.

He held out her chair and seated her. His manners were impeccable, and Wynne wondered what he'd do if she knocked over her water glass or used the wrong fork. She kept her eyes cast down toward her plate so he couldn't see her expression. Was she being unfair? It wasn't a crime to be well-mannered. She didn't know what was wrong with her.

Maybe Jake was right, and this was all part of her defenses. She didn't want to be hurt again, and Simon might be the man who could do it if she weren't careful. Putting her napkin in her lap, she turned to Skye, who was seated on her other side. As she chatted with her sister-in-law, she found herself listening with one ear to Simon's conversation with Max, who was seated across the table from him.

Her hostility rose the longer his cologne wafted around her. His deep voice grated on her nerves until she thought she'd scream. He had too much money and too much polish. And if she didn't know better, she'd think he was trying to annoy her on purpose. Why couldn't he hurry up and eat and get out of her hair?

Tomorrow was going to be a long day.

NINE

Simon's steps sank into the heavy carpet as he followed his cousin down the hallway. A faint paint smell emanated from the pale taupe walls, and he figured they'd been painted over the weekend.

The secretary ushered them into a conference room, gave them coffee and discreetly left them alone.

"I don't know what the big hurry was to read Jerry's will," Simon grumbled. "I've got more important things to do."

"Me, too. This shouldn't take long." Brian took a sip of his coffee and grimaced. "Tastes like it was made this morning."

Simon pushed his own cup away. He hated stale coffee, but he hated even more to wait. Drumming his fingers on the table, he crossed his legs.

Before he could complain again, Eric Wattrell came in. The attorney wore a black suit and pink shirt that made his cheeks look even more florid. His dark hair was slicked back, and he wore a perpetual expression of surprise.

He nodded at Simon and Brian. "Sorry to keep you waiting." Setting the sheaf of papers he carried down on the table, he pulled out a chair and sat down, then took a pen out of his pocket and arranged it precisely on top of the papers.

He'd always been too rigid. Simon suppressed a grin as he wondered what Eric would do if he stood and upended the table, sending his carefully placed papers flying across the room.

Too bad he couldn't do it.

Simon laced his fingers together. "Let's get this over with. I've got a lot to do."

"Quite." Eric adjusted his preppy glasses on his nose and pulled the first paper toward him.

"Were you aware Jerry changed his will?"

Simon and Brian exchanged glances. Simon put a question into his and Brian shook his head.

"When did he change it?"

"The week before he disappeared." Eric glanced down at his papers.

Simon wasn't sure where this was heading. "And?"

"And you are the recipient of his estate." Eric uttered the words as if they held great portent.

The weight of the pronouncement made Simon fall back against his chair. "What do you mean?"

"I mean Jerry's half of the business and all his personal belongings are to go to you. Which means, in effect, that with your existing ten percent, you hold a controlling interest."

"Guilt money," Simon muttered. He didn't know what to think. "It's not like there's anything to leave. The business is in the hole. But I suppose it made him feel like he was giving me something as he was taking my fiancée."

"That was Jerry for you," Brian agreed. "Always one for a grand gesture."

"Maybe it's for the best," Simon told his cousin. "I've been wanting to put some more money in the business and now I can easily do it."

Brian brightened. "Great! I've got some new design ideas."

At least Jerry's death had brought Simon and Brian closer, if that were possible. It felt good to be part of a team. But Rooney was going to have a heyday with this new information.

The white-capped waves bounced the boat on their crests, then let it plunge toward the bottom in a rhythm that Simon loved. He planted his feet on the polished deck boards and lifted his face to the sunshine.

"Makes it all worthwhile, doesn't it?" Wynne asked.

Joe cut the motor, and the yacht slowed then bobbed in the water like a duck. Simon lowered the anchor as a gull cawed, then swooped over the water as if to see if he'd thrown in a tasty morsel.

She joined him at the railing. "This is quite a ways

from where we last searched. Isn't this off the normal navigation path?"

"A bit. But the sonar looks interesting." There was something he couldn't read in her eyes, and he wondered if she thought he wasn't searching as hard as he could. He started to defend his hunch then shut his mouth.

Bjorn licked his finger and held it up to the wind. "Looks like we might have a gale today. We'd better make this quick."

Joe leaned over the side. "It doesn't look as deep here." He and Bjorn went into the bridge area.

Simon nodded. "The bottom is only about seventy-five feet down. But it's murky today from the waves." The light scent she wore was enticing. He stepped closer and drew in a deep whiff. "If I tell you that you smell like cotton candy, will I get smacked?"

She blinked and widened her eyes. "As long as you don't bite me, we're in good shape."

He grinned, and his spirits lightened when her smile widened. Though he knew she still didn't trust him fully, it would be an impossible situation to work together for the next few days with tension vibrating between them. Watching the wind toss her hair, though, he wondered if there would be more tension of a different kind between them with their spirits in unity.

"Look." She pointed to a boat roaring toward them. "The Coast Guard."

The Coast Guard boat slowed just off their bow and came to a stop. One of the men lifted his hand in greeting, and Simon did the same. The skipper maneuvered the Coast Guard clipper closer until they could converse.

"Something wrong?" Simon shouted over the wind.

"We'd like to board your boat." The other man's face was impassive. A dog barked from behind him, and a canine handler moved forward with the animal.

"What?" Simon couldn't imagine what could be going on. "We're looking for a sunken vessel."

"We've had a tip this might be a front for smuggling drugs," the officer said. His hand dropped casually to his gun.

"That's ridiculous," Wynne said. "Check out my qualifications and résumé. This is a legitimate venture. We're not some kind of criminals."

"You're not under suspicion, ma'am," the officer said. He moved forward and boarded the boat. The canine handler handed the dog up to him, and several other men followed.

Simon knew better than to protest. He clamped his lips together and folded his arms across his chest. "Go ahead and look. You won't find anything."

The head officer nodded, and the crew began to search Simon's boat. The dog went sniffing through the entire vessel. Bjorn and Joe exchanged angry glances with Simon, but neither objected when their duffel bags were searched.

It was nearly half an hour later before the Coast Guard was satisfied. Simon resisted the impulse to say, "I told you so," but he couldn't keep the smug smile from creeping across his face.

"You've delayed our work long enough that it's not safe to go down today," Wynne said. "The least you could do is tell us where this so-called tip came from."

The officer ordered his men back to the Coast Guard boat then paused at the railing. "It was an anonymous phone tip. We take all such calls seriously. I'm sorry for the inconvenience."

He didn't sound sorry. Simon didn't say anything. What good would it do? The damage to the day was done. The clouds and wind had increased, and they needed to get back to shore. Tomorrow was another day.

Once the Coast Guard departed, Joe started the boat's engine and began to motor toward the dock. They passed the quadrant Wynne had wanted to search earlier.

"Stop," Wynne called. Her brow was knit in concentration as she looked at the new computer screen.

Joe turned off the key.

Simon went to join her and Bjorn at the computer screen. "What is it?"

"There." She stabbed a finger at a smudge on the screen. "Doesn't that look like a boat? Here, see the cabin and the hull." She traced the outline on the screen.

"Sure does." He leaned forward. "It looks about the right size for the *Superior Lady*, too." This was no rock formation, he was sure. "But this isn't even in a likely place for it. It's more apt to be a fishing boat or something out here. There would have been no reason for Jerry to be in this area." He chewed his lip. "Unless..."

"Unless what?"

"See that island?" He pointed to a green smudge on the horizon. "Jerry used to use it for his trysts."

"You think Jerry and Amanda might have been heading there for a getaway?"

He shrugged. "Maybe. But I don't get why the boat went down out here."

A gust of wind shook the boat, and thunder began to boom overhead. "I'm going down, just for a minute," Wynne said. She grabbed her equipment and began to put it on.

"Five minutes, that's all we've got," he warned, snatching up his own equipment. "You realize this is stupid, don't you?"

"We'll be fine. The storm will hold off a few more minutes."

Simon wasn't as confident as she sounded, but he didn't want to leave without knowing what was down there, too. Moments later they both entered the waves.

After that initial dive, his fear had left him, and he had Wynne to thank for that. He watched her graceful movements as she moved through the water.

Near the top, the surf buffeted them, but under the waves, things calmed. He took the lead and torpedoed down toward the bottom. Wynne was right behind him.

He was still fifteen feet away when he recognized the shape of the boat. They'd found it. Simon grabbed Wynne's arm and pointed to the side where his floodlight illuminated the name: *Superior Lady.* He swam around the boat but didn't see any obvious reason for its sinking. It would take a more rigorous examination than the cursory look he could give it now.

Wynne pointed topside. He hated to leave, but he knew she was right. From down below, there was no way of telling how fierce the storm was growing. They had to get out of there. He glanced at his watch and realized they'd been down for nearly ten minutes.

They headed for the surface. As his head broke the water, he realized they'd miscalculated how strong this storm was. Waves crashed over their heads, and it took all his strength to make it back to the boat.

Joe grabbed his hand and helped haul him and Wynne to the deck. She was pale and panting by the time they both collapsed on the boat deck.

"We've got to get out of here," Simon gasped.

Joe nodded and went to the bridge. The engine fired right away and he headed the boat toward shore.

Simon grabbed blankets and wrapped one around Wynne and one around himself. The wind shrieked around them, and lightning flashed overhead. Simon felt responsible. He should have taken them to shore before diving. The GPS system pinpointed their find, and he could have come back the next day.

He glanced at Wynne beside him in the next seat. Her exultant expression said she was reveling in the storm. "You're not afraid?"

She shook her head. "I love weather. The power of God never ceases to amaze me. I feel close to Him in this kind of extreme storm."

"I'd say the thunderbird was mad we found the

boat," he said with a grin. "You think God is mad, too?"

"God is all about truth. I think He led us right to it."

She had faith in God. He liked that. "I'd say you're right."

The wind had torn the band from her braid, and Wynne's hair lay plastered on her head. She knew she had to look like a drowned puppy. Water ran in rivulets down Simon's face as he fought with the waves and tried to loop the rope to the dock.

He finally succeeded. "Come on!" He grabbed her hand, and they ran for his truck. He opened her door and got her inside then ran around to the driver's side. Wynne shivered in the cool of the truck. Her wet clothes stuck to her, and gooseflesh ran down her back.

"I'd like a hot cup of tea about now," she said, clasping her arms around her.

Simon reached behind the seat and produced a blanket and a thermos. "It's coffee and not tea, but it's hot." He unscrewed the cap and poured it out, then handed it to her.

She wrapped her hands around it and inhaled the aroma. "I'm not much of a coffee drinker, but I'd drink mud about now if it was hot."

"Some say that's what my coffee reminds them of." He grinned, and his dark eyes watched her.

She swiped a lock of wet hair from her cheek. "I must look a sight."

"Let's just say you wouldn't want to run into a reporter right now," he said.

"At least you're honest." She laughed and took another sip of coffee, then grimaced. "How much coffee did you use for this? I'm surprised it doesn't eat through the cup."

"I work long hours and need the caffeine."

"You must make it strong enough to eat the spoon." She wiggled her eyebrows at him. He didn't laugh as she expected.

His brows drew together. "What do you think that Coast Guard thing was all about? Anyone who knows me should know I'd never be a drug smuggler."

The way he said it made her wonder. "Why do you say that? Money is a powerful motivator for people."

"My mother was addicted to prescription drugs. I won't even take antibiotics. I see a natural doctor on the mainland when I'm not feeling well."

She could tell he was passionate about the subject. "I hadn't heard that. Maybe it was news to the Coast Guard, too."

"Who could have called them?"

His question lay between them for several moments. She didn't like the only answer. "Someone who didn't want us to find that boat. Did you tell anyone where we'd be looking today?"

He shrugged. "Sure. I talked to several people and mentioned it at the restaurant this morning. It was packed. Anyone could have overheard me."

"Who would have a motive to kill your cousin?"

"Half the women on the island." Simon leaned past her and rummaged in the glove box for a napkin. He wiped his still-dripping face with it then wadded it up and tucked it into the pocket on his door.

"Seriously?" She'd thought maybe the things she'd heard about Jerry had been sour grapes from men who felt upstaged.

"I'm dead serious. Jerry has left a trail of broken hearts from here to Rock Harbor. And there have been plenty of disgruntled old boyfriends—and husbands—to add to the carnage."

"Carnage. Strange choice of words." She grimaced at the oily taste of the strong coffee. "Was he malicious?"

"Jerry could be pretty brutal when he was done with a woman. More than one has shown up in tears at the boathouse."

"Why would he treat women like that?" The more she heard about Jerry, the more she disliked him. Could Simon be like that as well? Max and Becca had warned her against getting involved with Simon. They'd called him a heartbreaker, too.

"Why are you looking at me like that?" Simon's gaze searched her face.

"Like what?"

"Your eyes are squinty, and you look ferocious. I'd be scared to be in a dark room with you."

She couldn't help herself—a laugh bubbled from her throat. "Good. I think you could be as dangerous as your cousin." Simon had a way of penetrating her defenses, and she had to find some strategy to keep him at a distance. What that might be, she had no idea.

The lines at the corners of Simon's eyes deepened as he looked suddenly serious. "Not me, Wynne. I don't play around with hearts."

"You're saying you haven't broken any hearts—ever?"

He shook his head. "Women like my money, not me."

"I find that hard to believe," she blurted.

He gave a faint smile. "But that's because you're honest and straightforward. You say what you think and make no bones about where your interests lie. There's no doublespeak with you."

She thought it might be the strangest compliment she'd ever received. "Thanks. I think."

He grinned. "It's a refreshing change. Now if I bought a boat outrigged like Jacques Cousteau you might suck up to me to get a post on it."

"You might be right." She snuggled further into the blanket. "With that atrocious coffee in my stomach and this blanket I'm inclined to be generous and let you buy me some lunch."

"You don't want to change first?" He shook his head. "You really are an amazing woman."

"I'm not saying I wouldn't borrow your comb."

He chuckled and rummaged in the glove box again, then produced a comb with half the teeth missing. "It's the best I can do, I'm afraid."

"I'll take it." She took it and began to work the

tangles out of her hair. His gaze on her did funny things to her breathing. "Quit staring," she said.

"Sorry." He averted his eyes. "You've got the most beautiful hair."

"Yeah right, tell me that when it's plastered to my head." She quickly braided it again. "I don't suppose you have a rubber band or something around here?"

"Let me see." He sorted through the junk in the bottom of the glove box and produced a hair ribbon. "Will this do?"

She wanted to ask him why he had a hair ribbon in his truck, but she didn't want to know the answer.

TEN

Wynne glanced around the café and found nearly twenty sets of male eyes all focused on her. She doubted she had a stitch of makeup left, but at least she was wearing a sweatshirt that wouldn't cling when wet.

"I know I look like the lake's version of the Windigo, but would you all quit staring?" She smiled to take the sting out of her statement.

Most of the men had the decency to look away. She heard Simon's deep chuckle. "At least someone finds it funny." She stuck her tongue out at him, and his hazel eyes crinkled with amusement. As they moved to find a seat, she reminded herself to keep him at arm's length. It was hard when his good nature was so appealing.

She slid into a seat in the back. The men far outnumbered the women on the island, Becca had told her. Many of the women had moved away to find jobs and a larger pool of possible spouses.

Wynne glanced around the café. The bare planks on the floor had been scrubbed so many times there was only a trace of paint left on them. The sun and numerous washings had faded the red gingham curtains on the windows to a mellow pink. Old signs and banners decorated the walls, which were paneled with barn siding. Plastic red checked tablecloths covered the tables arranged around the room.

It felt homey and comfortable—or it would have if the men hadn't been staring. Wynne shifted in her chair and wished she'd put her back to the room. "Mind if we trade seats?" she whispered to Simon. "I feel like a guppy in a fishbowl."

He grinned and stood. "Too many piranha?"

Though he was joking, she could see the sympathy in his gaze. They exchanged seats, and Wynne felt more comfortable without seeing the men.

"They think they can look now that you can't see them." Simon chuckled and took his napkin, then laid it over his lap. "I can understand their fascination. You're pretty cute even with wet hair."

Her stomach did a slow somersault at the expression on his face. She wanted to look away and couldn't. "I have to look a mess," she whispered.

"Prettiest thing this side of the lake."

"That's not saying much," she said, finally breaking their locked gaze. "At least their stares can't turn my stomach."

The waitress brought menus. Her name tag read Rhonda. "Coffee?"

Wynne grimaced. "Thanks but no."

The waitress cocked an eyebrow. "Did you force some of that vile brew you make down her throat?"

"Guilty as charged." Simon looked unrepentant.

"Honey, I feel for you. No one can drink his coffee. Ours is better, I promise."

Wynne wondered how the waitress knew that. Rhonda was cute and perky. Had Simon used the famous Lassiter charm on her? Taken her home for a cup of coffee one night? She bit her lip. She needed to quit looking under rocks and take Simon at face value.

She laid down the menu. "Would you happen to have any hot cocoa? There's none on the menu."

"It's not on the menu, but you look like you could use a pick-me-up. We'll make some special."

While Rhonda went to get their drinks, Wynne glanced over the menu. She heard an intake of breath from Simon and glanced up. Simon's gaze was fixed on something behind her. She turned to see a man approaching their table.

"It's Alan, Amanda's brother," Simon muttered.

The navy suit he wore stretched too tightly across his massive shoulders and looked out of place among the jean-clad patrons of the café. His face was set and strained.

Wynne glanced back at Simon and saw the resignation in his face. Alan stopped at their table. Simon's face was closed and tight. Wynne could almost hear a palpable intake of breath from everyone in the room. It might have been her imagination, but she sensed the men lean forward to listen to the oncoming confrontation. From the look on Alan's face, this wasn't going to be a pleasant chat.

"I just came from your office," Alan said.

"Oh?" Simon glanced around. "Maybe we should take this discussion outside."

"You'd like that, wouldn't you?" Alan sneered. "You'd like no one to know what a murdering skunk you are."

"Simmer down, Alan." Simon half stood, and Alan shoved him back in his chair.

"I already called the sheriff, so don't think you can weasel out of this." Alan's face worked, and his mouth twisted. "You're going to pay for what you did to Amanda. And your own cousin as well! What kind of monster are you?"

"I'm just an ordinary man," Simon said, his voice weary. He rubbed his forehead. "Sit down, Alan, and we can talk."

"You might poison my coffee." Alan clenched his massive hands, big as boulders.

"Please, Alan." Wynne stood and spoke in her softest voice. She'd found lowering her voice when others raised theirs tended to diffuse some anger. The verse in Proverbs about a soft answer turning away wrath was very true. "Sit down."

"Did you plan this with him?" Alan's voice lowered a notch.

Wynne reached out and patted his hand. He snatched it away. "Sit down and tell us what you're angry about." For a moment she thought he would continue to stand and bellow, then he heaved a sigh and grabbed the back of the chair and jerked it out.

He plopped down and folded his hands over his chest. He directed his gaze at Simon. "Did you think no one would find out?"

"Find out what?"

Wynne thought she detected dread in Simon's voice, and she stared at him. An uneasy feeling started in her stomach. She remembered the sheriff had asked Simon about an argument he had with Amanda the day before she and Jerry disappeared. Her gaze swung back to Alan.

"Why you killed her."

"I didn't kill her, Alan."

There seemed to be a lack of conviction in Simon's voice. Wynne had her suspicions about Simon's feelings for his fiancée. She'd wondered if he'd been relieved when he thought Amanda had run off with Jerry.

Her gaze traveled to Simon. His stony face made her heart sink. She looked down at her hands. Though she wasn't sure if she could trust him or not, she wasn't about to incite Alan to more anger. Better to say nothing.

Simon forced himself to stay in his seat even though the accusation in Wynne's face made him feel like walking away. He couldn't deny he was disappointed in her. He had hoped she'd begun to know him well enough to know he wouldn't murder anyone. He took a gulp of coffee and burned his tongue.

He set down his coffee cup then looked up to meet Alan's angry glare. "You're right, Alan. Wynne is the one who found the boat. But that doesn't mean I wasn't looking as hard as I was able. I want to prove my innocence."

"That will be a trick after what I found out." Alan's voice was taunting.

"I suppose you found out your sister stole from me," he said quietly. Wynne gasped, and Alan's face reddened even more.

"You just wanted out of the engagement so you fabricated a lie."

"Why would I want out of the engagement? Our wedding was in a month." Simon hadn't wanted to think about that last day and certainly hadn't wanted to talk about it. He wished he could hide it in a closet in his mind and never open the door.

"Amanda wouldn't lie."

Simon looked at Wynne. He wanted her to believe him, needed her to trust him. "Amanda was my accountant, that's how we met. I had no reason not to trust her, but I'd received an audit notice from the IRS. I called an accountant on the mainland to review the books. He found over a hundred thousand dollars had been embezzled and traced it back to Amanda."

Alan was shaking his head as Simon talked. "Amanda wouldn't do something like that."

"She admitted it," Simon said. The memory swept over him.

Amanda wore a yellow sundress that showed off her tanned legs and arms. Her long blond hair cascaded to her waist, but Simon barely noticed her beauty now that he knew what the shapely exterior covered.

"Come in," he said. Amanda paused in the doorway of his office. The pounding of riveters made him wince. "Shut the door," he said.

"This sounds serious." She pranced in on stiletto sandals. Once she was seated in the chair across from his desk, she crossed one shapely leg over the other and gave him a bewitching smile.

Simon's lungs squeezed. "The report came back from the auditor's, Amanda. There's money missing." Would she admit she did it? He hoped she would. Maybe he could forgive her if she had a good reason for it.

Amanda's blue eyes widened. "You're kidding. A clerical error maybe?"

"No, no error. It's been embezzled. And Ben traced it back to you. Why would you steal from me, Amanda? I'd give you anything you asked." He waved toward the obscenely huge diamond she wore. "You wanted a fancy diamond, and I got it. You wanted a house overlooking Lake Superior and it will be done by our wedding. What possible reason could you have for this?"

At last Amanda's smile faltered. "You don't believe him, do you? You should know I wouldn't do that."

Simon leaned his face on his hands. "Amanda, he's got bank records. Don't lie to me anymore."

Tears filled her eyes, and her lips trembled. "I'm

sorry, Simon." She clasped her hands together tightly in her lap. "It was for us, for our future."

"What are you talking about?"

She told him what she'd used the money for, and rage began to burn in his belly. A sour taste backed up in his throat. "I see."

"I'm tired of having to ask a man for what I want. Just for once I wanted to be able to buy what I want when I want it and not answer to anyone." She lifted her chin and stared into his face. "Maybe I wouldn't even have to marry you if I had money of my own."

Something fragile inside him finally shattered with the defiance in her face. She didn't love him—she never had. "I see." He stood and went to stare out the window. From here he could see a hint of blue that was Lake Superior. He whirled around. "Then go! Make all the money you want. You're free of me."

She stood with her hand pressed to her heart. "Are you pressing charges?"

"I doubt I'll have much choice. The IRS is going to look at the books."

"You have to fix this somehow, Simon. Please. For the sake of all we meant to one another."

"What did we mean to one another, Amanda? I thought we had something special and now I find you just wanted my money. How do you think that makes me feel?" He still wasn't sure what he felt. He was numb.

"You'd better listen up, Simon. If I go down, you go down."

"What do you mean?" He felt too sluggish to be able to follow her.

"I'll implicate you, too. I'll say you had me do it, that this is something we cooked up together."

"For what purpose? The money was mine already."

"To cheat the IRS of taxes." She gave a self-satisfied smile. "Fix it, Simon."

"So you can live high on the hog?"

"Don't let jealousy get in the way of your good sense." She turned and rushed to the door and threw it open. "You'll be sorry if you dump me," she declared shrilly. "I'll still see you at the altar. If you don't show up, I'll tell the world how you made me do it."

She spoke loudly enough that he knew his receptionist had to have heard it. Bonnie had been with him for years, though, and she'd never liked Amanda. Wild horses couldn't drag this conversation out of her.

He watched Amanda run down the hall. Her sobs echoed back through the open door. He heard the door slam, and with the sound, his heart broke.

Alan's voice brought him back to the present. "You're not going to drag my sister's name through the mud."

"Amanda wasn't the darling you thought her," Simon said gently. He'd barely gotten the words out when Alan leaped to his feet and charged at him. The other man's bulk tipped Simon's chair over, and he crashed to the ground with Alan on top of him. He thrashed and managed to throw Alan off, then jumped up.

Wynne sprang between them. She put her hands on Alan's chest. "Sit down, Alan." Her voice was like a schoolmarm's, all authority and command. Alan tried to step around her, but she blocked him again. "You said the sheriff is on his way. Let him sort this out."

Just what Simon didn't want.

ELEVEN

The sheriff had herded them all into the backroom of the café, away from avid spectators. Wynne had offered to have Becca or Max come get her, but Simon had asked her to stay. She had to admit to herself she was curious. Her emotions raged between dread and hope.

She realized she didn't want Simon to be guilty. Just a few days in his company, and the walls she'd carefully erected around her heart were crumbling. Simon seemed full of integrity. If he was guilty of something as heinous as murder, then she might as well forget ever trusting her own judgment.

Sheriff Mitch Rooney's eyes were shrewd as he put one booted foot on a rung of the chair he'd pulled out. "Alan called me and said he had proof you murdered his sister. I'd like to hear it now."

Simon said nothing. He leaned back in his chair and folded his arms across his chest.

Rooney's gaze swiveled to Alan. "Well?"

Alan's hand shook as he pointed at Simon. "I talked to an employee who told me about the argument he had with Amanda."

"The mysterious fight." The sheriff took out a notepad.

Wynne could almost see the sheriff rubbing his hands together in his mind. He'd been out to prove Simon was guilty right from the start.

"The employee overheard Amanda scream at Simon and tell him that she'd make sure everyone knew what he'd made her do."

"What he'd made her do? That sounds vague. It could be anything." The sheriff glanced at Simon.

Wynne wanted Simon to speak and defend himself, but he continued to sit with his arms folded across his chest. His gaze connected with hers, and she nearly winced at his stony expression. He thought she was against him, too. She put a bit of pleading into her gaze, but he just looked away.

"You have anything to say for yourself?" Rooney asked.

Simon shrugged. "You already knew we'd had an argument. It had nothing to do with her death."

"What did you make her do?"

"Nothing. She had been caught in something she didn't want to take the blame for."

"I'm going to find out about this. You might as well make it easy on yourself and tell me."

Why was he holding back? He'd told Alan that

Amanda had embezzled from him. Why was no one saying it? She was tempted to tell the sheriff herself, but it wasn't any of her business.

Alan was chewing on his lower lip, and Wynne could tell he was torn between telling the sheriff what Simon had said and keeping it to himself.

The indecision on his face changed to a bullish determination. "He said Amanda had embezzled money. I say he killed her in a fit of rage. He should have known she wouldn't do anything like that."

Rooney's gaze sharpened. "Embezzlement?"

Simon sighed. "I don't want to drag Amanda's reputation through the mud now that she's dead. Can't you just take my word that this has nothing to do with her death?"

"I'm afraid not. I think you'd better come down to the station for interrogation."

"Are you arresting me?"

The sheriff hesitated. "Not yet. But I'd like an official interrogation on record."

"And if I refuse?"

Rooney's face darkened. "I'd hate to have to put out a warrant for you as a material witness. Might be embarrassing."

"For you or for me?" Simon shook his head. "I'm not going anywhere. Go get your warrant."

A darker flush traveled up the sheriff's neck and to his face. "You're not making any points here, Lassiter."

"I wasn't trying to. I don't have time to play games with you. I want to find out what happened to my cousin and my fiancée. I found the boat." An expression of consternation rippled across his face.

He shouldn't have said that. Wynne knew what was coming next.

The sheriff half stood, then sank back into his chair. "Give me the coordinates. You're not to disturb the site. We don't want the evidence contaminated."

"So you can railroad me in to a murder charge?" Simon shook his head. "I don't think so."

"You're impeding an official investigation. I'll see you in jail. How'd you find it?"

"Serendipity," Simon said. "You know Marquis Island? Wynne saw a blip on the sonar just offshore."

The sheriff looked alert. "Marquis Island? That's a known meeting place for Canadian drug smugglers. I should check out that angle."

Simon shook his head. "Jerry wouldn't have been involved in anything like that. Or Amanda."

"You never know," Rooney said, his chin jutting out. "At least it's something to check out. In the meantime, I need to look at that boat."

"Sheriff, I have a suggestion," Wynne began. "I've often worked with law enforcement agencies. Not many people are trained in deep water retrieval. I barely know Simon and have no bias in this case. Let me take charge of the process of raising the yacht."

Simon looked like she'd slapped him, and Wynne wanted to reassure him that she would handle things with the utmost professionalism. She bit her lip and looked away from his stricken face. The sheriff was still mulling over her words. She waited as the silence grew.

"I'll give you a list of references you can check," she said.

"I'll be in touch." Rooney released the chair and removed his foot from its rung. "And expect a material witness warrant shortly, Lassiter. You're going to tell me all about this."

"That's it? You're not arresting him?" Alan's face was mottled.

"This is all hearsay," Rooney said. "I need the name of the employee you talked to."

Alan shook his head. "I promised I'd leave this person out of it."

"Great, just great. You call me down here for something I can do nothing about. I have no real evidence."

"I'll get you the evidence," Alan shouted. He rushed from the room.

Rooney started after him then turned and looked back at Simon and Wynne. "I don't know what to think, Simon. Just come clean with me."

"I have been." Simon tried to put as much force into the words as he could to convince Rooney.

Rooney shook his head. "We're going to finish this discussion. You can count on it." He walked off.

Wynne looked at Simon. "This feels very personal to me. Does the sheriff have something against you?"

Simon sighed. "His sister worked for me for a while."

"That's it? That doesn't sound like much of a

reason to have it in for you." She could tell there was more to the story.

Simon rubbed his forehead. "She, uh, she killed herself when I had to let her go."

Wynne sucked in her breath. "Oh, my. That poor family. Why did you fire her?"

Simon's face was a stony mask. "She had a crush on me and had started following me everywhere."

"When did this happen?"

"A year ago."

Two women dead in a year's time. Wynne didn't want to doubt Simon, but the evidence was looking overwhelming.

Silence reigned in the truck as Simon drove along the rain-swept street. Water ran across the road in places, and he had to navigate slowly. Wynne had already tried him and found him guilty. He'd thought she would be more fair-minded than that. Disappointment hunched his shoulders and weighed him down.

He glanced at her from the corner of his eye. She was staring out at the storm that lashed the island. Maybe he should try to defend himself—tell her everything. He pressed his lips together. No, the less people who knew the full story, the better off he was. Once the sheriff knew the full scope of Amanda's treachery, no one would think he was innocent of her death.

He clamped his teeth over the words that wanted to spill out and drove Wynne back to Windigo Manor. The manor house seemed to hunker down in the wind and rain that lashed the brick exterior. Lights shone from the windows.

"The thunderbird is sure hitting us hard today," he remarked as he pulled the truck as close to the front door as possible.

Wynne nodded without looking at him. She put her hand on the door handle. "Wait a second," he told her. "Look, I don't want us to part with such heavy suspicion between us. I give you my word that I had nothing to do with Amanda's death."

"I want to believe you," she said softly. "But you have to admit it looks bad, Simon. You're asking me to trust you on faith alone."

"I think you know me better than you think, Wynne. You can't deny there's a connection between us."

He saw her throat move as she swallowed hard. "You trying to use that Lassiter charm on me?" she asked.

"There is no Lassiter charm," he said wearily. "I'm tired of hearing that. This is me, Wynne. A flesh-and-bone man with hurts and troubles like any other. I'm not some Prince Charming. Can't you trust me, just a little?"

"I don't know, Simon. I'm going to have to pray about this. I'm not sure we should work together anymore."

"But you were quick to offer your services to the sheriff, weren't you? You want to bring up that boat even if you have to stab me in the back to do it."

"That's not fair," she flashed back. "I'm trying to protect you."

"Some protection. You're throwing me to the wolves."

"Would you rather someone work on the project who is under the sheriff's thumb? At least you know I'll be honest."

"And how do I know that? Maybe Rooney has already got to you. You lived on this island when you were younger. Maybe you two are old friends."

"I'd better go in. You're being unreasonable." She opened her door and jumped out, then dashed through the pelting rain.

Thunder and lightning crashed overhead. Simon waited until she reached the front door then dropped the truck into gear. He put his foot on the accelerator, then with a sudden decisive mood, slammed it back into Park and turned it off. He got out of the truck and ran toward the porch. Cold rain stung his cheeks, but he hardly noticed.

He reached the front door and pounded on it, not bothering with the doorbell. He pounded again, and the door finally opened.

Max's frown lightened when he saw Simon. "I wondered why you didn't come in." His smile faded when he looked into Simon's face. "What's wrong?"

"Everything. The sheriff is about to arrest me for Amanda's murder. I need your advice. You got a minute?"

"Sure. Get in here out of the weather."

Simon followed Max down the hall. Looking into the living room, he saw a cozy scene with Becca, Gram and Wynne clustered around the baby. Wynne looked up and flushed when she saw him. He gave her a curt nod then strode past the doorway after Max. Let her wonder what he was doing here.

Max took him to his office. "Have a seat."

Simon realized he was tired to the bone. The emotional upheaval of the day had taken its toll. He sank into a leather armchair. "I'm not sure where to begin."

"How about with why the sheriff thinks you're guilty."

Simon nodded and began to tell Max the whole story. His friend nodded occasionally as he listened intently. He asked a few questions as the story unfolded. The relief Simon felt as he unburdened his troubles was as heartening as the first sign of spring to the U.P. He should have shared this with Max sooner.

"So what should I do?" he finished.

"The truth is always good," Max said. "God honors truth above all things. If you're wise, you get on board with what He thinks."

"The truth will land me in jail."

"I think it's a risk you have to take. Truth generally will win out."

"That's easy for you to say when you're not the one facing murder charges." Simon had thought Max would tell him to keep his mouth shut and find the real killer. This wasn't what he wanted to hear.

"As the truth comes out, the sheriff will be able to

follow leads to the real killer. As long as he's sure it's you, he won't be looking in the right places. You owe it to Jerry and Amanda to do what you can to bring their killer to justice."

Simon moved restlessly. "We don't even know for sure it was murder."

"Sure you do. Why else would your crew have been attacked and your equipment vandalized?"

"Maybe it was the drug dealers the Coast Guard was looking for."

"You don't believe that. Truth, Simon. Look for truth in all things."

"I'll think about it." But Simon wasn't sure he was ready to tell Rooney everything. He couldn't do anything from jail.

TWELVE

Wynne jiggled baby Isabelle on her knees as she waited for breakfast on the patio. She felt uneasy that morning. Since she and Simon had parted on such ugly terms, she wasn't sure if she should try to meet him at the dock or not. She wanted to find the truth.

"Why the long face?" Max asked, dropping into the chair beside her. Isabelle smiled and gurgled at the sight of her father. She reached pudgy hands for him, and Max took her and snuggled her against his chest.

"What did you and Simon talk about last night?" Wynne blurted out.

Max took a moment before he answered her. "You know I can't talk about a discussion that was in confidence."

"I don't know what to do. I want to trust Simon, continue the work. We found the boat, you know."

"I know."

"I saw a blip on the radar, and we stopped to check it out."

"You saw the blip, not Simon?"

His question brought up something she'd buried. She was the one who'd spotted the boat, and it had been found in an area Simon had discounted. Was it coincidence, or had he steered them away from where he knew the boat lay?

"I can see the wheels turning. What is it?" Max asked.

"Nothing," she said. The last thing she wanted to do was turn Max against Simon.

"Truth is always best," Max said gently.

Heat rushed to her cheeks. She bit her lip. "We found the boat in an area I'd suggested we search and Simon nixed. It was a fluke I was looking at the computer screen as we headed back to shore."

"And you think that makes Simon guilty?" Max shook his head and handed his daughter a rattle. "There's much more to this story than you know. Press Simon for the truth."

"I don't think he'll talk to me."

"You might be surprised."

"I'm not sure I want to get involved."

"You are already involved. Simon isn't guilty, Wynne. I can guarantee you that. This is one of those times when you have to trust your gut instincts. I don't believe you really think Simon is guilty."

"What if my gut instincts aren't very good? My track record is lousy when it comes to men. I think all men are like my brother, and don't see their faults until it's too late."

"Simon is as fine a man as I've ever met. You can trust him."

"I'm not sure I'm convinced, but I'll hang around for the endgame," Wynne said. She stood. "I'd better get to the dock if I'm going to catch a ride out to the site."

"Good luck. Becca and I will be praying."

Wynne lifted her hand in acknowledgement, then headed to her car. If she'd told Simon she was still a team player last night, he would have picked her up at the Windigo Manor dock. She just hoped she could catch him before he shoved off.

Saturday shoppers clogged the narrow streets of Turtle Town. Wynne parked in the gravel lot overlooking the bay, then hurried down the steps to the dock. She scanned the men along the boardwalk, but she didn't see Simon's familiar thatch of hair. Glancing around the moored boats, she spotted his boat. Good, she hadn't missed her ride.

She stepped over looped hanks of rope and fishing tackle boxes as she maneuvered to the boat. It bobbed in its mooring. There was no sign of life aboard. She stepped onto the deck. "Hello? Simon, are you here?"

She felt strangely uneasy. There was a waiting feeling on the boat, a presence that raised the hair on the back of her neck. She told herself she was being fanciful, but she wanted to flee. Forcing herself to take deep breaths, she moved toward the helm. Something crunched under her feet, and she looked down to find shards of glass on the deck. Her gaze traveled to the cabinet where the sonar equipment was stored.

The cabinet lock was busted, and pieces of the sonar were scattered on the deck. The computer monitor was smashed, the glass underfoot part of the monitor. Her blood began to pound through her chest, and she breathed in short gasps. Was the vandal still aboard?

She backed away from the mess as a figure came at her from the galley area. He wore a stocking over his face, but even if he hadn't, he moved too quickly for her to get more than just an impression of height and breadth. She put out her hands to ward him off, but he grabbed her with rough hands and shoved her to the deck then ran past her and jumped onto the dock.

Wynne felt the bite of glass on her backside and on her hands as she struggled to her feet. She looked down and saw one leg was bleeding from a cut on her calf. Tiny bits of embedded glass stung her hands.

She heard someone behind her again and whirled with her bloody hands held out in front of her. She felt a rush of relief when she looked into Simon's face.

His gaze traveled to her hands. "What happened to you?" He stepped onto the boat and grabbed her as she swayed.

She blinked to clear her blurry head. "An intruder. Look what he did to our equipment." Blood dripped from her palms.

"I don't care about the equipment." He took her arm and steered her gently to a seat. "Let me look at you." He grabbed a first-aid kit from a cabinet and began to clean her hands. "You're full of glass."

"He knocked me down."

Simon took tweezers and began to pull the shards of glass from her palms. Watching his head bent over her hands, she had to resist an impulse to lean down and lay her own head on his. He was a rock in times of trouble. She remembered what Max had said about trust and realized she had to let go of her distrust. If she went through life with her guard up all the time, she'd miss out on God's best.

"There. I think I got all the glass." Simon released her hands.

They still stung, though he'd covered them with a bandage. "You'd make a good nurse." She stared into his eyes. They were golden amber, not really brown. Warm and melting, his gaze knocked down the last of her defenses. She wanted to get to know him better. Maybe there was something there for them and maybe there wasn't, but she'd never know by hiding behind her fear.

"I need to call the sheriff."

She laughed. "It sounds like you'd rather face death than do that."

"Yeah, well I'm not in the mood for Rooney." He dug his cell phone out of his pocket and dialed.

She watched him as he told Rooney what had happened. She suppressed a smile at his anger. The attacker had better be glad he wasn't around.

Simon clicked off the phone. "He'll be here in a few minutes. You realize he's going to say I staged this." He sounded resigned.

"It wasn't you. This guy was thinner and shorter.

Strong though." She shuddered at the memory of how his fingers had bitten into her arms.

"Want a pop? I've got some in the cooler."

"Yeah, I could use a sugar jolt about now."

He leaned over to the cooler and fished out a dripping cola. She popped the top and took a gulp. Her hands had begun to throb, and the idea of crawling back into bed sounded tempting.

Simon nodded. "Here comes Rooney."

Sheriff Rooney put his notebook away. "I guess that's all I need."

"Are you going to find who did this?" Simon asked. Rooney had been surprisingly focused during the questioning. Simon wondered if he finally realized something else was going on.

Rooney pushed his hat back on his forehead. "I'll do my best. One of the deck hands tried to stop the intruder and got clobbered. He's still pretty shaken, but when's he's more coherent, maybe he'll remember something that will help. I think it might have something to do with that Canadian drug ring."

"Are you still kicking that dead horse? This has nothing to do with drugs!" Simon couldn't believe the sheriff was following such a stupid idea.

Rooney bristled. "There's nothing more promising unless you did this yourself."

"Sheriff, I saw the man who did this. It wasn't Simon."

Bless Wynne for her defense. Simon knew it would do no good though. Rooney wanted him to be guilty.

"I thought he had a stocking over his face," Rooney said.

"He did, but the size was wrong for it to be Simon."

Rooney just nodded and turned toward the dock. Simon knew he wasn't convinced that he hadn't hired someone to throw suspicion off.

"You're a poor excuse for a lawman," Wynne said. "Aren't you supposed to be impartial? Look, I'm sorry about your sister, but to be determined to make Simon pay by railroading him into a murder charge is inhuman."

Rooney stopped and turned slowly. "Don't talk about my sister," he spat. "I found her hanging from a barn beam. And he killed her no matter how he might have sugarcoated it to you."

Wynne's voice was soft. "I know you're hurting, Mitch. But don't let your grief corrupt your sworn duty."

Something flickered across Rooney's face before he swung around and presented his back to them. He didn't say another word as he rushed to the dock.

"Thanks for defending me, but I don't think you got through."

"You never know. I think he's going to look a little harder. I'm hoping he saw where his duty lies."

Simon sat beside Wynne and grabbed a pop for himself. "You never said what you were doing here."

"I came to help you figure out what happened to the boat." Her dark eyes were fixed on him.

He wasn't sure what he felt at the realization that she was ready to help him. "What about your misgivings? Did Max tell you what we talked about?" If Max had blabbed, Simon would kill him.

"No, no, nothing like that. Max and I talked, but he just told me it was time I listened to my gut." She grimaced. "My gut instincts have never been good, but I can't go through life fearful of trusting people."

"You can trust me, Wynne. I would never hurt you."

"That's what Max says, too. So I'm here to help. We'll get that boat raised and figure out what happened."

"We can't, remember? The sheriff says it's off-limits."

She grimaced. "Oh, yeah. Well hopefully they'll call me in as a consultant."

"I wouldn't count on it after the way you antagonized Rooney."

"I was just telling the truth."

Her voice was sounding stronger by the minute. For a while, he'd been wondering if he should take her to the hospital. Color was beginning to come back into her cheeks. "I'm not about to waste your expertise. You game to search for the Viking ship?"

She smiled. "I'll try to keep my sanity through it." She tipped her head back and studied his face. "You really think something like that is out there?"

"I know it." He was going to find it someday.

She sucked in her breath and stood. "Let's get out there."

"You're in no condition to go today."

"I'm fine. Anything is better than hanging around

with nothing to do. If nothing else, we could go back to that other ship we found."

She was right. "Okay. But you stay on board while I dive."

"You can't do that! You know it's not safe to dive alone."

"We don't have much choice. Look at your hands. I'll be fine." He nodded toward the hillside. "And here come the rest of our crew."

Joe and Bjorn hurried toward them. Joe reached them first. "Sorry we're late. I had engine trouble this morning." He glanced around the boat, then whistled. "What happened here?"

Simon told them about the intruder. Bjorn was scowling by the time he finished. "I should get my gun?" he asked.

"No, we're fine," Simon said hastily. Bjorn could be a hothead. The last thing he wanted was to be in more trouble with the sheriff. "I have a pistol on board." He'd make sure Joe or Wynne had it, though—not Bjorn.

Joe cleaned up the mess and scrounged up more equipment. He stepped to the helm and fired the engine. Bjorn untied the boat from its mooring. They headed out to the coordinates where they'd found the steamer.

Simon's spirits rose as Turtle Town fell behind them. Keeping an eye on the GPS, Joe got them to the coordinates. They didn't need the sonar with the site pinpointed.

"We're here," Joe said. Bjorn lowered the anchor.

Simon moved to the cabinet that held their gear. Wynne was right behind him. She grabbed her gear, too. "I'm going down with you."

"No, you're not." He took the gear from her and put it back in the cabinet. "I'll take a buoy with me. If I get in trouble, I'll send it up. You stay here and monitor things."

"How can I monitor anything with busted equipment?"

She had a point. He grinned. "Well, just put your feet up then. If I'm not back in two hours, come looking for me."

"Two hours in this cold water?"

"I've got a heavy dry suit. I'll be fine. I've dove that long many times." He began to pull on his suit.

"I don't like it." She was playing with her braid, a sure sign she was nervous.

"I don't, either, but we have to play the cards we're dealt. You already faced down one intruder today. I wouldn't want you to get hurt again. Whoever it was came on board when we dove before. He might try it again." He reached into the cabinet. "In fact, you'd better keep this close." He handed her a pistol.

"I don't know how to shoot." She held the gun awkwardly in both hands. "Is it loaded?"

"Yeah. Here's the safety." He showed her how to turn the safety on and off. "On second thought, I'll give it to Joe."

"Good idea. I'd likely shoot myself in the foot."

He stood looking down at her and an unexpected wave of tenderness swept over him. "It means a lot to me that you're here," he said softly. He could smell the fresh scent of her perfume. It was all he could do to stay where he was and not step closer to kiss her. How would those full lips feel beneath his? He wanted to find out.

With an effort he dragged his mind back to the search. "Say a prayer for me." He fell backward into the water and felt the cold waves close over his head. He dove slowly down to the steamer.

Windigo Wind looked just as he'd last seen it. Laying heavily on its side, it seemed as much a part of Superior as the bottom of the lake itself. It would make an interesting project for a few months.

And it would keep Wynne with him. The thought stopped him short. He didn't want her to leave the island. She'd become more important to him than he'd imagined.

He placed some markers on possible ports of entry into the steamer then saw a shadow and turned to see Wynne joining him at the boat. Her eyes were twinkling behind the clear glass of her mask, and he knew she hadn't been able to stay out of the excitement.

He sent her a stern look, but she just winked at him. The expression in her eyes always drew him in. It was a gut reaction that surprised him.

They swam around the steamer and planted markers of possible entry points to the interior of the boat. The project intrigued him more than he'd thought it might, and he realized it was because he was spending time with Wynne.

Working side by side in the clear water, they sifted through debris. He finally tapped his watch. They'd been down about an hour, and he was feeling the cold. Wynne had to be, too.

Wynne pointed up to the surface, and he nodded. They swam slowly up to the boat. As they neared the surface, he saw the hull of another boat near the *Thunderbird.* Kicking out more strongly, he shot the last five feet to the surface.

His head broke the water, and his gaze went to the other boat. Great. They sure didn't need Mike Wilson poking around their find.

"Ahoy, Simon," Mike called.

He wore a self-satisfied smirk that Simon wanted to knock off his face. "What brings you this way, Mike?" Simon asked, hauling himself to his boat. He turned and extended his hand to Wynne.

She grasped his fingers, and he helped her aboard then turned to face Mike.

"Sorry, boss, I tried to get rid of him," Joe muttered.

"No problem," Simon said softly.

"You were down a long time," Mike said his voice avid. "Anything I can help you with?"

"I think I've got it covered," Simon told him. The last thing he needed was Wilson butting in.

"I've got equipment you don't have," Wilson continued as though Simon hadn't said anything. "Let's partner together in this discovery. We can help each other out. I'll split it with you fifty-fifty."

"No thanks," Simon said.

Disappointment flared across the older man's face. "Have it your way," he said stiffly. He signaled the man at the helm, and his boat moved away.

Simon watched him go with a sinking feeling. "He'll be back. Wilson doesn't give up easily. I'd better file on this find before he does."

"Should we post a watch?" Wynne asked.

He shook his head. "I'm going back down to put out some buoys. That will mark it as our find."

"You think that will deter him?"

"It had better," he said grimly.

THIRTEEN

"Let's get some coffee," Simon told Wynne when they docked the boat.

"I'm game." Her bones ached from the cold.

She followed him to Bob's Eats. It felt as if buzz of conversation faded when they stepped inside. Maybe it was her imagination, but it almost seemed as though the men were staring at Simon. She thought she saw suspicion on several faces.

The waitress brought them coffee. "Sheriff's been looking for you."

Wynne didn't like the way Rhonda said it. She looked at the waitress with a question in her eyes.

Rhonda shrugged and glanced at Simon. "Better watch yourself, Simon. I hear he thinks he's got almost enough evidence to arrest you."

Simon looked stricken. As soon as the waitress was gone, Wynne leaned toward him. "We need to figure this out, Simon, before you end up in jail. Rooney is convinced it's either you or a Canadian drug ring. I think we're going to have to find the truth ourselves."

"I'm not quite sure how to go about that," he said.

"What about the old manager, Roger?" Wynne asked.

"What do you have in mind?"

"We could poke around his neighborhood, maybe talk to some of his employees. You said he started his own business. Shelby Boats, wasn't it?"

"Yeah." Simon was beginning to look encouraged.

"Let's see what we can find out."

They bolted down a sandwich then drove out to the neighborhood where Roger lived. An older man was out cutting the grass with a push mower. Simon stopped the truck.

"Let me ask the questions," Wynne said. She put on her most charming smile. Her size tended to be in her favor. She was so small, older men especially tended to underestimate her and treat her as a child.

The man returned her friendly smile. Dressed in a red gingham shirt and jeans, he looked to be in his sixties. "You lost, little lady?"

"I'm looking for the Shelby house," she said.

"You found it." The man nodded to a neat brick house with green shutters. "The Shelbys live there."

The man's friendly smile reassured her. "Oh, great. Have they lived here long?"

"Oh, 'bout ten years or so. Nice family."

It was time to probe more deeply. "Oh? I heard Roger has a bit of a temper."

"Don't we all?" The man grinned. "Are you with child protection services? The last one who was here was older than you."

Bingo. There was more to Roger than they'd seen so far. "No, I'm not with the agency. Has he been investigated for mistreating his kids?"

The man's open, friendly look began to fade. "Nothing major. I'm sure Roger is a fine father. He spends a lot of time with his kids." Suspicion began to creep across his face. "Who did you say you were?"

"Thanks for your help," Wynne said hastily. She hurried back to the truck and told Simon what she'd found out. "It sounds like he's got quite a problem with his temper."

"That still doesn't make him a murderer."

"No, but it sure makes him a likely suspect," Wynne said. "Any man who would mistreat his kids is capable of anything."

Simon looked grim. "True." He glanced at Wynne. "You want kids?"

"I didn't use to think so, but since Isabelle has come along, I'm beginning to think I might."

"I love kids," Simon said as he put the truck in gear and drove away from the curb. "I was an only child and I always wanted a brother and a sister. I wouldn't mind having a whole houseful."

Wynne glanced at him from the corner of her eye. His good nature and patience would make him a good father. She stifled a gasp at the mental image that came to her mind of her and Simon around a dinner table with three children. Where had that come from? She needed to watch herself or she was going to get hurt.

Simon turned and looked at her. Was that a wistful look in his eyes? His pensive smile did funny things to her insides. She glanced away and looked out the window.

"We're not far from Jake's. You want to stop by?" he asked her.

She nodded. "I was just thinking about that. I didn't want to ask."

"You can ask me anything, Wynne. You've gone out of your way to help me. I'd do just about anything for you."

The unexpected note in his voice brought her gaze back to him. What she saw in his gaze dried her mouth. She wasn't sure anyone had ever looked at her with that expression of longing and tenderness.

What was developing between them? She was almost afraid to examine it. The feelings that stirred in her heart were unlike anything she'd ever experienced. And it was all moving too fast. Did that mean it was just infatuation?

She cleared her throat and looked away. "Do you know how to get to Jake's?"

"Sure." He turned on Jake's street. "It's the yellow house with blue shutters, right?"

"Yes." She leaned forward in her seat. "Jake and Skye are outside."

Her brother and sister-in-law were sitting in a yard swing. Jake's arm was around Skye, and they were deep in conversation. Skye was looking up at Jake with an expression that warmed Wynne's heart. She loved to see Jake and Skye so happy.

Wynne and Simon got out of the truck. Jake turned his head at the sound of the truck door. "Hey, what are you two up to?"

"We were in the neighborhood and thought we'd stop by and make sure you were taking good care of Skye," Wynne said. She hugged her sister-in-law.

"Want some iced tea?" Skye asked.

"Sure. But stay put. I'll get it." Wynne went inside while Jake and Simon dragged yard chairs from the garage. The aroma of apple and cinnamon drifted to her nose from the candle on the mantel.

Wynne peeked into the nursery. Jake had painted it a pale yellow and Skye had done a mural of Noah's ark. The tiny animals frolicking on the painted meadow looked so lifelike.

Wynne heard a sound and turned to see Skye behind her in the doorway. "This is so darling, Skye."

"I love it. Now if this baby would just get here." Skye rubbed her stomach.

"One more month."

"You sound wistful. Your turn will come." Skye's smile faded. "You're spending a lot of time with Simon."

"It's just a job," Wynne said.

Skye laughed. "I don't believe that for a minute. You were off the lake hours ago and you're still together. I'm not blind. I see how you look at him and how he looks at you. There's something going on there, Wynne, whether you're willing to admit it or not."

Wynne put down a stuffed bear she was holding. "Maybe. How did you know for sure Jake was the one?"

Skye looked pensive. "Jake made me feel safe and alive all at the same time. I knew I could trust him with my heart and my life."

It was easy to see that ability in Jake. Simon made Wynne feel like that, but she wasn't sure she could trust him like she trusted Jake. Why was she so frightened to trust? Maybe it was because she felt it so deeply this time. She knew if Simon betrayed her in some way, she might never recover.

This feeling she felt uncurling in her chest was different than anything she'd ever experienced. But also scarier. And that was the real problem. It was one thing to venture beneath the water and explore. It was something else to be willing to explore the depths of feelings she'd never had.

Skye smiled. "You look terrified. I know the feeling."

"You do?"

"Sure. With feelings this big, you know if you lose it the hole it will leave might swallow you up. But step out in faith, Wynne. I think God brought the two of you together."

Wynne was beginning to think Skye might be right. She followed her sister-in-law back outside where they talked for a while. The women made spaghetti and garlic bread for dinner, and it was nearly nine o'clock by the time Simon drove her home.

"I had a nice time tonight," Simon said, turning the truck off in front of Windigo Manor.

The moon shone on the lake, and Wynne could smell the fresh scent of the water through her open window. "Me, too," she said. "Thanks for going to Jake's with me."

His arm was along the back of the seat. With a slight movement, he caught a lock of her hair in his fingers. "I love your hair," he murmured. He leaned over, brought it to his lips and kissed it.

No one had ever kissed her hair before. Before she could respond, Simon pulled her toward him and bent his head. His lips found hers in the darkness. She put one hand on the smooth fabric of his shirt.

He tangled his fingers in her hair and dragged her closer as he kissed her. The scent of his skin, the tenderness in his lips and the touch of his hands in her hair caught her up in a cauldron of emotion. She clung to him as a tidal wave of longing swept her up.

When he finally released her, she managed to drag in a breath. She put her fingers to her lips. "I don't think I've ever been kissed quite like that before," she whispered.

His breath whispered across her face. "Me neither." His voice was husky. "And don't accuse me of using charm on you. You're a special woman, Wynne."

She didn't know what to say. "I'd better go in," she finally said after a long pause. She still didn't move.

If only she could hold on to this moment. All her doubts about how she felt seemed insubstantial in the light of the storm of longing that had swept over her.

She wanted Simon in her life, but she was afraid to let him know. Scrambling out of the truck, she dashed for the house. She heard Simon shout something, but the wind snatched the words away.

Simon drove toward his house. He was tired, but elated as well. His heart still raced from the kiss he'd shared with Wynne. He loved just sitting and watching her expressive face. Today she'd shown her courage and pluck.

She didn't have to dive today after being attacked but she'd insisted. Did that indicate her attraction to him? He was afraid to analyze it.

He turned down his street and noticed car lights coming up fast behind him. Keeping an eye on the approaching vehicle, he found himself pressing the accelerator. The other car zoomed up behind him and rode his bumper, something Simon hated.

He tapped his breaks to warn the other vehicle to back off, but the car began to edge around him. Simon pulled to the left, nearly onto the shoulder. This wasn't a good place to be pulling such shenanigans. The night was pitch-black. The road hugged the cliff that looked down on waves that crashed onto rocky shores. One false move and it would be easy for a car to go over the side.

Fuming, he clenched the steering wheel with both hands. "Just go around," he muttered.

The car drove beside him, then with a sudden movement it crashed into the side of his truck. Metal screeched against metal, and Simon fought to keep from skidding in the gravel along the shoulder. The tires screamed, and he gritted his teeth and struggled with the careening truck.

The other car slammed into him again, and he realized for the first time that the other driver was deliberately trying to run him off the road.

He jerked the wheel to the left and slammed into the other car. The other vehicle swerved and barely missed the rocky outcropping on the other side of the road. Simon jammed on his breaks and pulled his truck onto the shoulder. The other car sped away.

Simon tried to read the license plate but it was too dark. He didn't recognize the vehicle, either. But someone had just tried to kill him.

The grandfather clock in the hall sounded twice—2:00 a.m. Wynne flounced on the bed and punched the pillow. She hadn't been able to sleep since Simon called to tell her someone had tried to run him off the road.

It only gave more credence to the thought that Jerry and Amanda had been murdered. Wynne wondered what the sheriff was discovering about the sunken boat. Why would anyone have wanted to kill them? Jealousy maybe? And why was the killer targeting Simon? Or was Simon the target all along?

Maybe she should ask Simon for a list of Jerry's old

girlfriends and ask more questions. She pummeled the pillow again and rolled over. Her fingers crept to her lips. Just thinking about Simon made her lips tingle all over again.

She heard a sound and saw a shadow flit by her open door. Recognizing her sister's shape, she sat up. "Becca, is that you?"

Becca poked her head in the door. "Shhh, you'll wake the baby."

Wynne lowered her voice. "Sorry." She patted the bed. "Want to gab a little like we used to?"

Becca bounced onto the bed and giggled. "Max will wonder what happened to me." She flopped on the other pillow and slipped under the quilt. "I wanted to talk to you anyway. You were glowing when you came in tonight. Anything you want to tell your big sister?"

"Big sister? I'm the older one."

"But I'm bigger," Becca said smugly. "You're a shrimp."

"Thanks a lot," Wynne said dryly. She wanted to talk to Becca about Simon but didn't know how to begin.

"What's up with you and Simon?" Becca asked after a comfortable silence. "When you came in tonight, you were glowing."

Wynne's cheeks burned. "Glowing? I think you're exaggerating."

"No, I'm not. And you were dreamy-eyed all through the rest of the evening. Did he kiss you?"

"Nosy, aren't you?" Wynne laughed and put her palms on her hot cheeks.

"He did, didn't he?" Becca clapped her hands. "Oh, dear, I'm going to wake up the baby."

"Okay, he did," Wynne admitted. Instead of Becca crowing, her sister went silent. "What?" Wynne demanded.

"Are you going to hurt Simon?"

"I thought you and Max were worried about him hurting me? Was that just hype to get me interested in him?"

Becca sat up. "No, no. I was concerned, but now I see how vulnerable he is. And you're so driven, Wynne. Your career is everything. Can you imagine living on Eagle Island and not going off on a new adventure?"

"For the first time I'm actually considering what that might be like," Wynne admitted in a low voice. "The thought of leaving for Australia isn't very attractive, and I was really excited before I came here." Was she losing her drive? Had meeting Simon changed her that much?

Her sister went silent at her admission. Then she cleared her throat. "You've got it bad, big sister," she said softly.

Becca wasn't telling Wynne anything she wasn't already beginning to suspect herself.

FOURTEEN

Simon acted as though nothing had happened between them. Wynne tried not to feel disappointed. What had she expected—for him to hold her hand and make eyes at her? She told herself to grow up.

When they reached the *Windigo Wind* coordinates, Wynne looked out over the white caps. "Where are our buoys?"

Simon frowned. "You're right, they're gone. There was no storm last night."

They looked at one another. "Wilson," Wynne said slowly. She pulled on her dry suit and fins, then went overboard. Kicking down through the clear water, she got to the boat before Simon. He joined her moments later as she stared in dismay at the boat. Someone had begun salvage on it. A hole had been knocked into the hull.

Simon glanced at her then swam inside the steamer. Wynne felt too heartsick to join him. The best stuff was likely gone. Wilson must have been very determined to have come out here at night.

After a few minutes, Simon joined her and they swam slowly back to the boat. When her head broke the surface, she spit out her mouthpiece. "He's stripped it, hasn't he?"

"Yep," Simon panted. "I'm going to file a complaint. I'd clearly marked it with buoys in accordance with maritime law."

"All you can do is take him to court and it's a long process. He knows he won't have to answer for it," Wynne sputtered.

"Yeah, I know." Simon sounded resigned. "Let's get our gear and do what we can."

They worked until nearly four o'clock, taking half hour breaks to warm up. Wynne found interesting artifacts still in cabinets and other rooms, and her initial anger began to fade. They would have to post a guard to keep Wilson out though.

She and Simon climbed aboard for the last time that day. Wynne squeezed water out of her hair, then wrapped it in a towel. She felt as cold as Superior in a January blizzard. The June sun was not enough to ward off the bone-chilling effect of Lake Superior's depths. She snuggled into her terry sweats and sat beside Simon.

He gave her a weary smile. "I had no idea archaeology was such hard work. It's not much like Indiana Jones."

"The movies tend to romanticize things," Wynne

said, her smile widening. It was a common misconception. And marine archaeology was especially challenging since the scientist was working in an unnatural environment.

"You did a good job today," Wynne told him. "Tomorrow will be better. You'll have some idea what you're doing."

Joe joined them. He sat beside Simon and propped his bare feet on the dash. "Want me and Bjorn to stand guard tonight?"

"If you're up to it," Simon said.

Wynne listened to them talk and watched the white foam that rolled over the tops of the endless blue water. She spotted a boat moving toward them. With a start, she recognized Mike Wilson's boat. "Speak of the devil," she said. She sprang to her feet and threw a tarp over the artifacts they'd found that day. Hopefully, Mike wouldn't get close enough to see, but she was taking no chances.

The other boat drew nearer, and Mike hailed them. His portly figure was clad in an all-white outfit she assumed he thought looked dapper, when in reality, it made him look even rounder.

"Any luck today?" Mike called.

She wanted to launch into a tirade, but Wynne forced herself to smile sweetly. "A little," she said.

Simon was scowling. "I clearly marked my find with buoys, Wilson. You had no right to try to horn in on my find."

"I don't know what you're talking about," Mike

protested. "I'm just out looking for a ship to salvage." His gaze wandered over the deck and landed on the tarp. "What you got under there?"

"Don't play dumb. I know you're the one who knocked a hole in the hull of the *Windigo Wind*. I've marked the find again. If I have to, I'll get a lawyer to keep you out."

"You don't have to be quite so hostile. I just wanted to offer my assistance. If you need help with anything, remember my rates are quite reasonable," Mike said, turning back to the helm. His stiff back proclaimed his outrage.

"We'll keep you posted," Simon called. "That man bugs me big-time," he muttered as Mike's boat moved off in the waves.

"He won't get nothing again," Bjorn said grimly. "Me and Joe will make sure of that."

Simon nodded. "I'll join you and we'll take watches through the night."

"You'll be too tired to work tomorrow," Wynne objected.

"We don't have much choice."

"Don't do it because of me," Wynne said. "This isn't such a valuable find that you need to wear yourself out. We could look for your Viking ship tomorrow."

Though she felt weak with fatigue, she forced a smile. "Let's get back in the water." The cold chill had eased, and she glanced at her underwater watch. "We've got a few more hours before sundown."

He glanced into her face. "At least your lips aren't blue."

His gaze lingered too long on her lips. And she felt herself swaying toward him. She took a step back. He blinked and turned away, and Wynne felt a stab of disappointment. Maybe last night's kiss had been a fluke, a mild flirtation on Simon's part. The last thing she wanted to do was make Simon think she was after him.

She turned and pulled her dry suit back around her shoulders then zipped it up. Swimming back down to the site, she forced herself to focus on the steamer.

After awhile, Simon touched her hand, and pointed to his watch. She looked at her own and realized they'd been working nearly two hours. No wonder her muscles ached from the cold. Fatigue overwhelmed her as she swam toward the boat with the sack of artifacts.

Her head broke the surface of the water, and she looked over the rolling waves. Where was the boat? She turned and looked the other direction. Nothing. Hypothermia made her thought processes slow. Had they drifted with the tide to a different place? But no, that was impossible. The archaeological site hadn't moved, so they'd been in the same place. It was the boat that had moved.

Simon's head surfaced. He pulled his mask from his face. His lips were blue, and dark circles showed under his eyes. He blinked the water from his eyes and looked around. "Where's the boat?"

"It's not here," she said. What a stupid thing to say.

Of course it wasn't here. Simon could see that for himself.

Simon's eyes widened, and he tread water as he flailed in the water and turned in a circle, his gaze searching the horizon.

A few moments later, his frantic movements slowed. "Let's think this through."

His words sounded slow and lethargic in Wynne's ears. She knew they were in a desperate situation, but hypothermia made her feel listless and uncaring. She pulled off her gloves and dug the nails of her right hand into her left wrist. The pain sharpened her senses.

Simon's eyes kept closing, and he jerked them open again. She reached out and gripped his arm, then snatched the glove from his right hand and pinched the skin of his wrist between her fingernails. His eyes snapped open, and she saw a more alert awareness surge over his face.

"Thanks," he muttered. "We have to figure out how to get out of this. We'll both be dead in another fifteen minutes."

"I know." Her gaze raked the horizon again, but all she could see was a distant white speck from a sailboat.

"I've got a flare," Simon said suddenly. He put his glove back on, and his hand plunged into the water as he fumbled with the bag at his waist. He pulled out a flare gun. "Pray." He shot the flare into the air.

Wynne watched the white flash arc into the air then burst into color. She tried to pray, but her mind was slowing again. *Help, Jesus,* was all she could formulate.

Time seemed to slow to a crawl. The waves grew, or maybe she was just sinking deeper into the cold clutch of the water. Waves slapped her in the face, the numbing cold too familiar now to rouse her. A warmth began to creep into her limbs, and she realized in some dim recess of her mind that this would be the end.

"Stay awake," Simon said, his voice slurred. He took her hand, but she was too numb to feel it.

"I'm trying," she mumbled. At least she thought she said it. Simon didn't answer, and she looked into his white face. His eyes were closed, and he was listing to one side, barely keeping his head above water. She touched his face, and felt a touch of regret. They might have had something between them, but it was going to be too late.

Simon's limbs felt pleasantly warm, and he imagined he was swimming in Hawaii. A beautiful white beach beckoned, and he could sense the warm sun on his face. It was just a little ways off. All he had to do was swim to it, and he could lay on the shining sand. He moved his arms and leg feebly. He heard Wynne's voice as if from a great distance.

"Come with me," he slurred. He tried to take her hand, but her head was sliding under the waves. A last remnant of cognition caused him to understand she was drowning, and he grasped at her arm, tugging her toward the surface. Her white face looked like death. He cradled her head in his arm and tried to pray but it was hard, so hard, to formulate thoughts, much less words.

The last thing he remembered was a voice shouting off to his left.

When he awoke, he was wrapped in a solar blanket. His teeth chattered, and his legs and feet felt like they were on fire. Wynne. He tried to sit up, but his muscles wouldn't obey him.

He weakly turned his head, his gaze searching for Wynne. Another form lay on the deck by his left side. All he could see of her was her black hair spread out on the deck. Her face was turned away. A blanket was snugged around her, too. He tried to see if she was breathing and saw a faint rising and falling of her chest.

"Wynne," he whispered. There was no response from the still figure beside him. He tried to reach out and touch her, but it was going to be some time before he could move. He wet his lips. "Wynne," he croaked.

She sighed and her head lolled around toward him. Her face was as white as the foam after a storm. Her lips were still blue, and her eyes were unfocused.

"Simon?" she whispered.

Her voice was so faint he had trouble hearing her even though she was only a foot away. "I'm here," he said.

"Where are we? I thought we were dead."

It was a good question. Simon had no idea how they'd cheated death, but he wanted to find out. He tried to move again, and found his muscles a little more cooperative. He managed to sit up and look around.

They were on a sailboat. One lone figure crouched by the engine. The sails had been lowered, and the boat sped through the water. Simon turned and looked and realized they were just offshore from Windigo Manor.

The man at the helm saw him. "We'll be ashore in no time," he shouted above the sound of the motor and the wind.

Simon recognized him as one of the owners of the new condo complex on the other side of the island.

A few minutes later, the boat bumped the dock at Windigo Manor. The man took a whistle and gave several short, shrill blasts then hurried to where Wynne and Simon were on the deck.

"How did you find us?" Wynne asked. She blinked, and awareness sharpened in her eyes.

"I saw the flare. You were both really lucky." The man grabbed another blanket and wrapped it around her. "What happened to your boat?"

"That's what we'd like to know." The boat. Now that Simon could think again, the magnitude of losing the boat hit him. And what about Joe and Bjorn? Had something happened to them?

"Do you need another blanket?" Gram asked anxiously.

"This is perfect. I'm warming up now." Wynne had finally stopped shaking, and she felt warm and lethargic. She didn't want to think about their close call. All she wanted to do was snuggle under the covers with baby Isabelle. She wanted to savor every second of her life.

Becca paced across the living room rug. "Max and Jake are out looking for the boat with Simon. You don't have any idea what could have happened to it?"

"None. It was really weird. I just hope the other men are okay. What if someone threw them overboard and they drowned?" Wynne shivered at the thought.

Gram patted her hand. "I'm sure they're fine. Maybe the anchor broke."

"They still had the engines and the GPS system to stay put," Wynne pointed out.

Becca turned away, but not before Wynne saw the worry in her sister's face. "Is there something you're not telling me?" she asked slowly.

"No, no, of course not." Becca thrust a cup of hot tea into her hands. "Here, drink this."

Wynne wrapped her cold hands around the warm cup, enjoying the heat that crept into her fingers. She took a sip and closed her eyes at the bliss of the hot liquid sliding down her throat.

"I think I'll go check on dinner," Gram said. "Call if you need me."

Once their grandmother was out of the room, Wynne glanced up at her sister. "How did Simon look?"

"Fine. You know how guys are. Too macho to let on that anything can hurt them."

"You think he was hurt?" Wynne tried and failed to keep the alarm from her voice.

"No, he's fine. I meant he acted like what you'd both gone through was no big deal. Typical male." Becca brushed the hair back from Wynne's face. "You scared me to death. I thought you were dead when they brought you inside."

"You can't get rid of me that easily." Wynne leaned against her sister's hand.

"Max had to practically drag Simon out to look for the boat. He wanted to hover over you. Once the doctor said you'd be okay, he finally went with Max but it was with obvious reluctance. I think he's smitten." Becca smiled, but the worry didn't lift from her eyes.

The front door banged, and they both looked to the doorway. Wynne recognized Simon's heavy tread in the hall, and her heart rate sped up. How ridiculous that he could do that to her when she felt too weak and shaken to sit up.

The worry on his face eased when his gaze found her. The concern for her she saw in his eyes warmed her. "Find the boat?" she called, forcing more of an upbeat tone to her voice than she really felt.

"Nothing yet. The Coast Guard is out looking, too."

The way he was staring at her did more to warm her cold insides than the hot tea and blankets had done.

Max followed Simon into the living room. "He was pretty useless. He kept yapping and worrying about you." He grinned as Simon turned red.

Wynne pretended not to notice, but her cheeks went hot, and she knew they were just as crimson as Simon's. "What about Joe and Bjorn?"

Simon's confused grin faded. "No sign of them."

The doorbell sounded, and they heard the sound of the sheriff's voice in the hall. "Maybe he has news about them now," Wynne said.

FIFTEEN

Simon felt like a schoolboy with his first crush. Even with the sheriff bringing possible news, he couldn't stop looking at Wynne. He'd thought he'd lost her today, that they would both die. Something about nearly dying made a man appreciate the things that really mattered.

He turned to face the sheriff as Rooney came into the living room. "Rooney, any news of my boat?"

Rooney looked sober. "Yeah, we found it, but there was no sign of Joe or Bjorn."

"Maybe the boat broke down and someone took them aboard?"

"We're checking on that. The engine wouldn't fire so it's a possibility."

Simon moved restlessly. "What are you doing to find them?"

Rooney shrugged. "The usual. The Coast Guard has copters and planes out. But it's been hours."

Simon nodded. They both knew Superior's cold embrace killed quickly. As it had nearly killed him and Wynne. If Joe and Bjorn were in the water, they were dead. He silently prayed for God to lead someone to his men and that they were alive.

The sheriff cleared his throat. "The autopsy came back and Jerry and Amanda both died of drowning."

"That doesn't mean it wasn't murder," Simon blurted out.

Rooney raised his brows. "You're right. Maybe I was wrong about you. And about these attacks on you—any idea who hates you?"

"You might talk to Wilson. With me out of the way, he could plunder the boat all he wanted." Simon swiped his hand over his forehead.

Rooney nodded. "I'll check it out." He glanced at Wynne. "Your girlfriend's comments made me realize maybe I was letting our history color my judgment. I'm trying to be impartial. I have divers checking out the sunken yacht." Rooney glanced to where Wynne still sat snuggled in blankets. "I'd be glad for your help, Miss Baxter."

"Of course," Wynne said softly. "Call me when you need me."

"We should have a team together in a few days."

"Sounds fine."

Simon glanced at Wynne, and their gazes connected. It was as if she touched his mind and heart when she looked at him. Their near deaths had strengthened the bond between them. Wynne looked pale and spent, and Simon curled his fingers into his palms. He'd like to get his hands on whoever had stranded them out in the cold water.

Max walked the sheriff out, and Simon sat next to Wynne. He took her hand. "Your fingers are still cold," he said.

She curled her hand into his. "I'm fine. What do you think really happened out there today?"

"I wish I knew. It could be that the anchor broke and the engine wouldn't fire so it drifted away."

"You sound like you don't believe that."

"I don't. You were attacked today, and we've had several other problems. It felt too deliberate today."

"I think so, too. We've got to get to the bottom of this. What about Wilson? With your boat out of commission, he could plunder the boat without interference."

"Maybe." Simon didn't like Wilson, but the man didn't seem like a murderer, and whoever had taken his boat had almost succeeded in killing them both. And maybe already killed Joe and Bjorn.

"Let's go talk to him in the morning," Wynne suggested. "Maybe he'll reveal something."

"I wouldn't count on it." Simon knew Wilson was too wily to admit to anything.

Max came back in. He carried his baby daughter, and Becca trailed behind him. They both sat down in the chairs by the window.

"I think we could use some prayer power," Simon said. "I don't know what's going on, but God does."

"I was about to suggest the same thing," Becca said.

They all bowed their heads and Simon prayed for wisdom and guidance in the days ahead.

Wynne hopped in the truck as soon as Simon stopped in front of Windigo Manor. Her heart surged when she saw Simon's face. The care and concern in his eyes warmed her.

"I saw Wilson at the dock," he told her. "We'll have to move fast or he'll be out in the boat before we can talk to him."

Right straight to business. Maybe the care she saw on his face was a trick of the light. Or wishful thinking. She told herself to work on figuring out what happened to the boat and ignore her love life. Or lack of it.

"Any word on Joe and Bjorn?"

"Nothing yet." His voice was tight.

She touched his hand. "Don't give up hope yet. They might have made it to an island or been picked up by a boat."

He didn't answer, and she knew he thought she was being naive. And maybe she was, but she wasn't ready to assume the men were dead.

Simon drove in silence to the dock. "He's still there," he said, his voice relieved.

Wynne saw Mike Wilson standing on the dock next to his boat. "How are you going to handle it?"

"I don't think it matters. He's not likely to admit to anything. But at least he'll know we suspect him and maybe he'll back off."

He had a point. "Okay." She got out of the truck and followed him to where Mike stood talking to a big man in bib overalls.

"Hi, Mike," she said, forcing a note of cheeriness into her voice.

Simon shot her an incredulous look then folded his arms over his chest. "We're on to you, Wilson. Stay away from my boat."

Mike held up his hand. "I suppose you're the one who sicced the police on me. They were on my doorstep this morning before I even had my coffee. But lay off. I haven't intruded on your site."

"Yeah, right," Simon said. "I suppose you didn't tamper with my boat, either."

A calculating expression crouched in Mike's eyes. "The cops said your boat was out of commission." He gave a weak smile. "Sorry to hear about that. We could team our resources. I'm still open to that idea."

"I have another boat I can use," Simon said. "You may have slowed us down, but you didn't stop us."

"I have no idea what you're talking about," Mike sputtered.

Wynne decided she'd better jump in. "Where are Joe and Bjorn? Did you take them off the boat?"

"I don't have time for this nonsense," Mike said. He released the rope and hopped aboard the boat. His face was tight with anger.

"We didn't accomplish much with that," Wynne said.

Simon's cell phone rang, and he dug it out of his

shirt pocket. "Lassiter," he barked. His voice changed as he listened.

Was that relief on his face? Wynne was afraid to hope. She held her breath as she listened to Simon.

"At least they're okay," Simon said. He clicked off his cell phone and looked at her. "They found the men. They were picked up by a passing fishing boat on its way to the mainland."

"What happened?"

"Two men boarded the boat and attacked them. When they came to, the radio was smashed, the anchor chain cut in two and the boat set adrift. Joe tried to start the engine, but it wouldn't start. They drifted for hours before they were picked up. Rooney had someone look at the boat. There was sugar in the gasoline and the spark plug was missing. Guess whoever did it wasn't taking any chances of us having spare parts."

Wynne flinched. "Do you think whoever did it realized we were still down?"

"I think they would have had to." Simon's voice was grim.

Wynne put her hands over her face. "I'm scared, Simon. We almost died."

His arm slid around her waist, and the spicy scent of his cologne slipped up her nose. His nearness comforted her. She leaned against him and buried her face in the rough fabric of his shirt.

"Hey, we'll be okay. God's in control of this. We'll figure it out." His other arm encircled her as well, and they stood like that for several long minutes with his chin parked on the top of her head. She could have stayed like this forever. Simon made her feel protected and secure. The sensation felt foreign. But nice—very nice.

She finally sighed and pulled away. "We'd better go. Do we need to do anything about getting Joe and Bjorn?"

He shook his head. "They're catching the ferry back."

"What do we do now?"

"I'd rather not go diving until we get Joe and Bjorn back. They'll be on guard now. We could slough off today and do nothing."

"Or we could see what we can find out about what's going on," Wynne said. "What about Amanda's brother, Alan? Could he have done this or do you still think it was more likely to have been Mike?"

"I have no idea." Simon's voice was weary and resigned. "Nothing makes sense. Let's take the day off. Maybe go see Brian. I haven't even checked in on the shipyard to see how things are going."

"Let's go there first, then we can see what Alan has to say." A smile lifted Wynne's lips. He wanted her to tag along. He could easily have dropped her home, but he took it for granted that they'd spend the day together.

He took her hand as they went toward the truck. Wynne thought the sun suddenly shone brighter and the blue sky turned brilliant. The thought that someone might be trying to harm them seemed suddenly ridiculous.

Simon drove to the boatyard and parked in the lot that held five other vehicles. The sound of hammering echoed from the side yard. A few workers milled around three large boats in various stages of completion.

"I don't see Brian," Wynne said.

"We'll check around back. He's generally out here somewhere. The boy works too hard, especially with Jerry gone. He thinks everything rides on his shoulders."

Wynne pointed. "There he is." A small boat on props held Brian's rapt attention. She thought it looked like a dinghy. "Pretty small boat he's working on."

"We build whatever the customer wants. Beggars can't be choosers."

"Is the business really that bad?" she asked Simon as they skirted piles of lumber and made their way toward Brian.

"It's pretty bad. I'll be surprised if we make it to the end of the year. Jerry was the spark in the business. Since his disappearance, the sales have died."

"I hate to hear that. Poor Brian. What will he do if the business goes under?"

"I don't even want to think about it," Simon said. He lifted his hand in greeting. "Hey, Bri. How's it going?"

Brian paused and wiped the perspiration from his brow. His smile did little to lighten the worry in his eyes. "I was beginning to think you'd deserted us."

"We've had a few problems of late." Simon explained what had been happening with the search. "Did you need me here?"

"Not really, I was just rattling your chain. Things are fine." Brian's voice was overly hearty.

"New sales?"

Brian hesitated. "Not really. But I've got a few leads."

"Sounds great."

Listening to the men try for a positive note made Wynne wish she could do something. Would any of her colleagues be in the market for a new boat? She could make a few calls and see if she could drum up some business. She hated to see Brian handed another blow. Simon could weather the storm just fine—he had plenty of money. But Brian seemed the type who would be lost behind a desk. He belonged outside with a hammer in his hand.

"I think I'll take a look at the books." Simon glanced at Wynne. "You want to keep Brian company? I'll just be a few minutes."

"Sure." Wynne hopped on top of a two-by-four on a pair of sawhorses. "What's this you're building, Brian?"

His eyes lit up. "It's going to be a motorboat for a man on the mainland. I'm designing it to be faster than usual." He pointed out the lines of the boat.

Wynne watched the animation on his face. He certainly knew his subject.

He broke off and blushed. "Sorry. I tend to go on and on. I know it's boring. You're getting a glazed look on your face."

"No, I find it interesting," Wynne protested. "It's great to be so passionate about your work."

"Like you are about marine archaeology," Brian said. "How long will you be here?"

"Until the end of August."

Brian frowned. "You don't sound excited. I thought you were looking forward to it."

"I was." Wynne looked away. "I like Eagle Island."

"Get out while you can. The Thunderbird puts her claws in you and you're trapped here for life."

"You could leave if you wanted to."

Brian gave a brief smile. "I'll never leave, just like Simon won't. This island is in our blood. There's no place like it."

Wynne knew Simon's opinion, but she was curious about what Brian thought. He surely knew the boat better than anyone else. "Tell me a little bit about the yacht that sank. Do you think a design flaw could have caused it to go down?"

Brian hesitated. "I know Simon doesn't think so, but you never know about a boat until it's tested. I tried to tell Jerry not to go out without another boat along in case of a problem. He thought he was invincible."

Wynne saw the pain on his face. "Any idea what could have gone wrong?"

"Not really. Now that the boat's been found, we should know more soon. Are you going to help raise it?"

"If they need my advice, I'll give it."

Brian propped his foot on a boat prop. "You and

Simon seem awfully chummy. What's going on with the two of you?"

Wynne's face burned. "We're friends and colleagues."

"I think it's more than that. Just be careful, Wynne. I like you, and I don't want to see you get hurt."

Wynne decided to abandon all pretense of disinterest. Brian knew Simon better than anyone else. "Why do you say that? Do you think Simon will hurt me?"

"I shouldn't have said anything. I'm sure you're different from the rest." Brian cut his glance away. "Here comes Simon now. Forget what I said. I don't want Simon mad at me."

He sounded almost afraid of his cousin. Wynne had to wonder why.

SIXTEEN

They didn't find Alan at home, and someone in town said he'd gone to the mainland for a few days. Wynne resolved to keep Simon at arm's length. She'd been discounting the warnings until she spoke to Brian. She needed to remember she'd only known Simon a couple of weeks.

At church that next Sunday, he sat with her then joined the family for Sunday dinner. The afternoon seemed to drag on forever for Wynne. She wanted to believe Simon was the steady, thoughtful man he appeared, but with all the warnings, she didn't know what to believe anymore.

The *Thunderbird* was repaired and the men returned to work by Monday. For the following week, they'd worked on the sunken steamer. Wynne was beginning to get used to the coldness of the water. They'd set out at daybreak that morning and had been working underwater for an hour.

A school of freshwater cod paused to inspect Wynne's work, and she smiled at their inquisitiveness. No storms had swept through, and the clarity of the water was superb. She estimated visibility at close to a hundred feet. A perfect day for work.

She paused and hovered at the boat bow, then dug out her small shovel and began the tedious work of releasing the *Windigo Wind* from its watery grave. She dumped debris into a bucket, and when it was full, swam a few yards away and deposited the dirt on a mound that had been growing over the past week.

She glanced around and saw Simon hard at work on the other side of the bow. Storms had piled dirt and debris around the boat nearly up to its deck. She wished they had more help.

She began to dig around the hull again. Some of this debris looked like it had been buried a long time. The storm must have violently churned up the floor of the lake. Her shovel hit something, and she dug it in more deeply. It didn't feel like rock. She used her fingers and pulled dirt away from the item.

It finally came loose. She picked up a small looped and formed piece of metal. For a moment she couldn't place what it was. She turned it around in her hands. It looked strangely familiar. She'd seen something like this before. She brought it closer to her mask and studied it.

Her eyes widened when it finally clicked. A Viking belt buckle of a common type. It couldn't be. Excitement began to shimmer along her spine. She waved and tried to attract Simon's attention, but he was intent on his work. Her fingers clutching the buckle, she swam to him. She touched him on the shoulder, and he looked up.

She opened her hand and showed him the buckle. He took it and examined it. She didn't know if he would recognize it or not. Then his head jerked up, and she saw his eyes widen through his mask. They had to go topside and talk about this. She pointed up, and he nodded.

She swam up toward the boat, and Simon shot past her. By the time she hauled herself aboard the yacht, he had his mask down around his neck and was studying the buckle.

He looked up as she knelt beside him. "Is this what I think it is?" His voice shook.

She took it from him and rubbed some of the corrosion away. "It's a Viking belt buckle. Bronze and fairly common."

"You've discovered what I've been searching for years to find." He sounded almost jealous.

"It was a fluke. If you'd been working on my side of the *Windigo Wind*, you would have found it."

His shining face clouded. "Have we disturbed it too much with our work around the steamer?"

"I don't think so. I've sifted every bucketful we've moved. But any new storm could disturb things as well so we have to work fast. I'd like to call in some help, some of my colleagues."

"Can't we do it more quietly than that? If the press hears about this, it will be a zoo."

Wynne tried to think of another option. She desperately wanted help on this. It was too important to mess up. "Maybe Jake could help. Though we'd likely kill one another before a week was out."

Simon's eyes narrowed then he grinned. "I have a feeling your tongue could whip any man into shape."

"You act like I'm a shrew."

"Not a shrew but maybe a goose, honking and fussing for her way until the exhausted male sees the light."

She wanted to be mad, but she could tell he was teasing, and she burst into laughter. "I'm surprised you haven't found a new partner if I'm bothering you that much."

"It's kind of endearing," he said.

The amusement in his eyes brought a lump to her throat. She turned away from the expression in his gaze and looked back at the buckle. "I wonder what else is down there?"

"I can't wait to find out."

"What about the steamer? We've come a long way on it."

"It's not going anywhere. Let's get what Viking artifacts we can, then continue to investigate the steamer. We'll be moving the debris from around it as we go anyway."

"True. And once it's free, we'll lift her out of the way and see what's under her." She was getting more excited just thinking about it. This was a huge find. For decades, there had been speculation that Viking ships had made it this far before Columbus ever discovered America. A discovery like this could turn history on its head.

The weather turned cold so fast up here, they wouldn't have long to fully excavate. Once autumn moved in, storms could bury the site again. Of course, she would be in Australia by September anyway. The thought was strangely disquieting. She was beginning to love it here. All the feelings of belonging that she'd felt coming to the island as a child had surged again. It would be hard to leave.

She glanced at Simon. Once she was gone, would he miss her at all? Sometimes she was surprised to see an expression in his eyes that brought her heart to her throat. She didn't examine it too closely because she didn't want to face what it might mean.

"We've got most of the day. Want to get to work or should we call Jake in now?"

"I think I'd rather talk to him in person. Let's do what we can ourselves today. I'll contact him tonight."

Simon was cold and tired by the time the day had ended. They had found no other artifacts, but they'd moved a lot of dirt and debris from around the hull of the *Windigo Wind*.

Wynne had pulled on terry sweats, but her lips were still blue, and her face looked pinched.

"I think spending so much time in this cold water is too much for you," he told her. "You don't have any fat to keep you warm."

"I'm used to it."

"You're used to warmer water. Gitchee Gumee has a cold embrace." He grabbed a blanket out of the cabinet and tossed it to her. She caught it and threw him a grateful smile. The blanket enveloped her, and a hint of color began to come back into her pale cheeks.

"Want some coffee?" Steadying herself against the pitching of the boat as it moved through the waves to shore, she got out the thermos.

"You're braving my coffee? You must be cold."

"I'd drink strychnine if it was hot. And your coffee almost qualifies." She grinned at him and poured coffee into a foam cup.

He took it when she handed it to him and inhaled the scent. He'd tried to weaken it when he'd made it that morning and it smelled watered down to him. She poured herself a cup as well. Her movements were graceful, and he enjoyed watching her. He'd never met someone who was so completely at home on a boat.

With Joe at the helm and Bjorn working on sifting dirt they'd brought up from the bottom, Simon settled into the chair next to Wynne. He wished she'd talk about herself. The stories she could tell of her excavations would be riveting. Most women enjoyed talking about themselves, but Wynne had a deep affinity for people. She was a good listener. Still, he'd never really quizzed her. Maybe she'd open up if he did.

"Tell me about your last dive."

"You were there. What do you mean?"

"No, I mean in Spain."

Her face lit up. "My friends try to shut me up when I get started. You sure you want to hear this?"

"I'm fascinated by history and what can be found. If it gets too much for me, I'll let you know."

"I was excavating a Spanish galleon off the Spanish coast. We found several chests of treasure." She rattled on about doubloons and a cannon.

Her hands joined the expressiveness of her face, and Simon was drawn into the world she described. He could almost see the barnacle-encrusted cannon and masts she'd found. Why had he never pursued his real passion like she did? It took courage to go off and do something so out of the realm of normal life.

He'd been lazy, living on the island and following in his father's footsteps. A yearning to see and experience more stirred inside. He had the education. He'd minored in archaeology, where he first discovered his passion for Viking remains. But there was no reason he had to confine his interest to that period. He could get more schooling if he needed to, then find a job on a team like Wynne's.

Maybe on her team. The thought of her leaving the island in a few weeks disconcerted him more than he expected. He was getting used to having her around. But was that all it was? He was beginning to think his heart might be in danger. His relationship with Amanda had drifted toward marriage because it was something Amanda wanted. He'd chosen the easiest course of action then, just like he did with his career. He didn't want to make that same mistake again.

Close proximity to Wynne was different. She seemed to have no interest in him as a man. He'd better guard his heart or he'd find himself yearning for a woman who wouldn't give him the time of day.

The boat dock appeared ahead, and he gladly relinquished his thoughts. Wynne shrugged off the blanket and went to tie up to the piling. The scent of fish from the nets spread on the dock wafted in the light breeze. Shouts of children fishing along the dock and the hum of other engines sounded familiar and common after their exciting find.

What would everyone think when they heard Viking artifacts had been discovered? He realized the find wouldn't change anyone's life on this island. Men would continue to fish the lake, the fish canneries would continue to operate, tourists would still come to the quaint little town of Turtle Town.

Simon felt suddenly overwhelmed by how small his life was. Yet he'd been content, until now. Had Wynne opened his eyes?

"You're looking at me weird. Do I have dirt on my nose?" Wynne rubbed her face. Her lips were full of pink now, instead of blue, and her eyes were bright. It hadn't taken her long to recover from Superior's cold grip.

"No, I was just lost in thought." He joined her on the dock. "Want to get some dinner? I'm starved."

"Why don't you come home with me? Dinner will be on the table by the time we get there."

"Should we call ahead and warn them?"

"Moxie will fix plenty. She's the most efficient housekeeper on the island. There's always too much food." Her flip-flops twacked against the soles of her feet as she followed him toward the truck.

Wynne stopped and he almost barreled into her. "Sorry."

"My fault. I think I see Jake's head in the window of the diner. Maybe we should talk to him now."

"Yeah." Simon wasn't eager to bring someone else in on their project, and he realized it wasn't only because he didn't want to share the find, or his building the relationship with Wynne. But they had no choice.

Wynne ducked into the café. Sure enough, Jake was seated by the window. Wynne stopped in the doorway and smiled at her brother. "Skye will have your hide if you're late for dinner. What are you doing here?"

"She's getting her hair cut, and I'm killing time."

"She's not cutting her hair off, is she?" Wynne asked, her voice full of alarm.

"No, it's just a trim. Though she's been talking about hacking if off when the baby comes."

Simon's gaze wandered to Wynne's long braid. He'd hate it if she cut her hair. The realization that he had an opinion about it startled him. A woman's haircut was generally the last thing he noticed.

The waitress approached. Eagle Island was too small not to know pretty much everyone. Christy was the daughter of one of Simon's employees. She'd hung around the office all last summer before he became engaged to Amanda. She was pretty in a vaporous sort of way.

"Can I bring you some coffee?" Christy asked.

She batted her long lashes at Simon, and he looked away. No sense in encouraging her.

"We have a project that might interest you," Wynne said. "Scoot over and I'll tell you about it."

"Great." Jake moved over for Wynne to join him in the booth.

Simon sat across from them. Was Wynne avoiding sitting beside him? He'd noticed she'd been withdrawn a little over the last few days.

"What's up?" Jake folded his hands in front of him. He glanced at his watch. "Make it snappy. I have to meet my lovely wife in fifteen minutes."

"This." Wynne opened her palm and showed him the buckle. She'd been eager to see his reaction. Jake used to eat, sleep and dream Vikings when they were teenagers. He knew more about them than most people.

He picked it up reverently. "Where'd you get this?"

"In Lake Superior."

"You're kidding!" His voice was avid. "Viking origin, probably fourteenth century." He stared at her. "Are there any more?"

"Not yet. That's where you come in. We need some help to excavate the site before autumn storms start."

Christy was still hanging around the table. "I'll help, too," she put in eagerly.

"That would be great. Are you sure you have time?" Wynne's voice was gentle.

Simon studied Wynne's face. Her smile to the younger woman seemed genuine. He thought he detected pity in her gaze. Though he hated to bring more people into the project, Christy could be an asset. She was a quick learner and had helped out in his office during her summers all through high school.

"I'm a teacher's aide at the elementary school so I'm off for the summer. I've been bored, and this job is the pits. This will be great."

"Great. I'll show you how to sift through the buckets of dirt. You can do that aboard the boat while we're diving." Wynne looked at Jake.

"Are you in?"

"Do you even have to ask? This is too exciting a find to pass up." His eyes gleamed.

"You have to keep this quiet," Simon warned.

"No problem. I'll only tell Skye."

"I won't say anything," Christy promised. Her voice vibrated with excitement. "But would someone explain why this is so exciting?"

"It could prove Vikings were really here before Columbus," Jake said. "There have been other artifacts found, but they've all been questionable in some way—either outright hoaxes or items that could be explained in another way. This could change what we know about how far the Viking longboats could travel."

"When do we start?" Christy chirped brightly.

"Tomorrow at eight," Simon said. He could hardly wait.

SEVENTEEN

Dinner was over, and night had settled in. "We should go out on the lake tonight and look for the northern lights," Wynne said. "They're supposed to be really great this week. Clear skies and great visibility."

"I want to go," Molly said, taking her father's hand.

Max looked worried. "I'd planned to write for a while tonight."

Becca sighed. "You're always writing."

"I know. My deadline is in three days though. I'll make it up to you," Max promised.

"There's no reason the two of you can't go," Becca said. Her eyes gleamed.

Wynne knew what her sister was thinking. She started to refuse but Simon was nodding his head. "We might as well. You game, Wynne?"

"Sure." The word popped out of her mouth before she could stop it.

"Can I go?" Molly asked hopefully.

"If your mom says it's okay." Wynne tried to signal with her eyes to let her sister know it would be good to have Molly along.

"It would be awfully late for you," Becca said. "I doubt you could stay awake that long."

"Please, Mom." Molly grabbed Becca's hand and gave her a soulful look.

She'd called Becca "Mom" since the wedding. Her own mother had died when she was small, and she'd loved Becca from the first day she arrived at the manor. It did Wynne's heart good to see her sister so happily ensconced in the island life.

"She can take her sleeping bag. If she gets tired, she can crawl in there," Simon said.

Wynne wondered if he was as uncomfortable as she at the thought of being alone under the stars. They spent a lot of time underwater alone, but it was hardly the same thing.

They'd been moving closer, then pulling apart for days now. It was getting to be uncomfortable, and Wynne didn't know what to expect, or even what she wanted.

"You're sure?" Max asked.

"We'd love to have her along," Wynne assured him. She could only hope Simon didn't sense how much. At least with Molly along, she could keep her growing feelings from showing. The child would be a great distraction.

"Yay!" Molly danced around the living room.

"Go get a jacket and your sleeping bag," Becca told her. "And brush your teeth before you go."

Molly raced out of the room and up the staircase. "I'd better get a jacket, too," Wynne said. She hurried to her room and went to the bathroom off her suite. Looking in the mirror she nearly groaned. Gram had tried to tame the wild locks, but tiny wisps of hair had escaped and stuck up all over her head. New freckles mocked her from their position on her nose, and it was peeling from the sun as well.

Good thing it would be dark. She glanced at her watch. If she was fast, she could take a shower. She turned on the hot water and raced through lathering her hair and body. She threw on clean jeans and a red top, then put on a touch of makeup and braided her wet hair. Twenty minutes later, she grabbed a jacket and flew down the steps.

Her gaze met Becca's, and Wynne saw the smirk on her sister's face. She narrowed her eyes at Becca in warning. Her sister clamped her mouth shut and looked away. Wynne hurried to ward off her sister's giggles.

"All ready," she said. "I still had dirt in my hair so I took a quick shower." She prayed Simon wouldn't realize she wanted to look nice for him. She was as bad as the other women who mooned over him. Self-disgust made her smile stiff as she took Molly's hand and followed Simon outside.

She didn't want to go. Simon could tell by the fake smile on her face. His earlier anticipation faded. Oh well, they could just go out for a little while and he could plead fatigue and bring them back before Wynne made it any more clear she wasn't interested in spending time with him if it didn't pertain to her research.

Molly chattered all the way to the dock, but neither of the adults said much beyond answering her in monosyllables. As they neared the waterfront, he saw flashing lights and people swarming the pier.

"What is it—what's wrong?" Wynne leaned forward in her seat.

Simon saw a glow of red. "Fire!" He gunned the engine and drove down the hill to the dock. There was a sour taste in his mouth. Even before he got close enough to tell for sure, he knew his yacht was on fire.

He was right.

Adrenaline surged as the engine exploded on the boat and shot flames high into the air. He heard a fireman shout, "Get back!" The crowd surged toward the truck, and Simon had to slam on his brakes to avoid hitting a pedestrian. He pulled off the road and slammed the gear into Park.

"Stay here," he barked as he jumped out of the truck. He pushed through the throng of people and got as near his boat as he dared. He spotted Alan a few feet away. The man had a satisfied expression on his face.

Simon rushed toward him and grabbed him by the arm. "You did this!" He wanted to smash his fist into the man's face.

Alan wrenched his arm free and held his hands out in front of him. "I had nothing to do with it. But it's justice, don't you think?"

Simon clenched his hands. "Someone set this. My yacht didn't just burst into flames for no reason." He felt a touch on his arm and whirled to see Wynne and Molly.

Wynne's face was white. "I'm sorry, Simon," she whispered.

All the fight left him, and his shoulders sagged. "Everything is gone. All my notes, my equipment."

"I know." She reached up and drew him to her shoulder as if he were a child.

Though she was tiny, barely reaching his chest, he managed to fold himself down into her embrace. He could smell the clean scent of her shampoo and the fragrance of her perfume. He wrapped his arms around her and reveled in her comfort. They fit together like they were made for each other.

The stray thought made him pull back. He'd never believed in the idea of the fates of two people being intertwined by God in that way, but Wynne was changing his mind. He dropped his arms and turned back to talk to Alan, but the man had disappeared.

Sheriff Rooney appeared from the middle of a group of firemen. His face grim, he saw Simon and came toward him.

Rooney nodded at Wynne, then his gaze settled on Simon. "Everyone okay, Lassiter?"

"Yeah, we're okay."

Rooney nodded. "I've been interrogating witnesses. No one saw anything." He rubbed his chin. "I'm beginning to wonder if you should hire a bodyguard."

Simon grimaced. "At least you're not accusing me of arson. I'll be okay. Just figure out who's doing this."

Rooney nodded. "I'm doing my best." He wheeled around and went back to join his deputies.

Simon watched him go. "I think he's disappointed he won't have my company in jail."

Wynne grinned. "You always look on the bright side." Her smile faded. "What are we going to do?"

He shrugged. "I've got my pick of boats at the boatyard. What equipment do we need for the excavation?"

"Just shovels and five-gallon pails. Some old screens will work to sift the dirt." She slapped her head. "Our GPS is gone. Can we find the site again?"

Simon nodded. "I've got the coordinates down in my notebook." He patted his pocket. "Here it is."

"Whew, good thinking."

"I wasn't taking any chances." He glanced around. "I guess there will be no watching the Northern Lights tonight."

"I'm tired anyway," Wynne said. She glanced down at Molly. "And I think this young lady has had enough excitement for the night."

"That was cool," Molly said. "I'm sorry about your boat though, Simon."

He ruffled her hair. "Me, too, muffin." He sighed. "This might slow us down a few days."

"Nope. You get the boat, and I'll get the rest of the equipment. I'll meet you at the dock at, say, ten?"

Simon's hope surged back at the energy and confidence in Wynne's voice. "We're not letting whoever this is beat us." He saw a familiar face and lifted his hand. "Brian, over here."

His cousin rushed up to him. His face worked with emotion. "What happened, Simon?"

Simon shrugged. "Someone torched my boat. I'll have to get another one."

"You're going on with it?" Brian looked panicked. "I lost my brother, and I don't want to lose you, too, Simon. Let it go. The sheriff will figure out who did this. That's his job."

"I think we're going to have to figure this out. We're missing something," Simon said. "I've found the Viking trail, and I'm not letting it get away. A storm could wash it all away. We have to strike now."

Brian's mouth gaped then he closed it and gulped. "You found Viking remains?" He shook his head. "I thought you were nuts. Can I help?"

"We can use all the help we can get." He quickly explained about finding the Viking belt buckle.

"What about the steamer? Maybe we should move it to see what's underneath."

"It would help to get it out of the way," Wynne put in. "We'll be careful."

"Count on me," Brian declared. "We're going to find who did this and bring them to justice."

Simon hoped his cousin was right. It was hard to imagine how a murderer lurked behind familiar faces. And he still had to find a boat to use.

EIGHTEEN

The tugboat bounced along the waves. Wynne couldn't remember when she'd seen a sorrier piece of floating junk.

Simon noticed her glance around the helm and gave her a shamefaced grin. "It was the best I could do on short notice. We had one yacht done, but it didn't have enough deck space to work. I begged this from a friend in town."

"Beggars can't be choosers." She propped her bare feet on the dash. The red glint of her toenails in the sunshine pleased her. She rarely took the time to paint her nails, but she'd been restless last night after the destruction of the boat.

"You've got the smallest feet I've ever seen," Simon said. "Did your parents bind them when you were a kid?" He grinned and turned the boat to head out to open water.

At least he said it in an admiring tone. Wynne

decided to forgive him for remarking on her size. "I used to think I must be adopted since I was so much smaller than Becca and Jake. Then my mom had me look in the mirror with her, and I could see I was a miniature version of her. I have no idea why I'm the shrimp of the family."

"Maybe you didn't drink your milk."

She smiled, then her gaze traveled to Christy, Jake and Brian standing at the railing. Joe and Bjorn were at the helm. "At least we have more help today. I'm eager to get down there. You, me and Jake can do the diving and let the others sift through the mud and debris."

"I wish we had time to do it all. They may make some of the better discoveries." He glanced at the sieve with an envious expression.

"Sharing the glory is never fun, is it?" She put her feet back down and jiggled her knees.

"Are you nervous?"

"A little. I was just thinking about the destruction of the boat. Can we talk about Jerry and Amanda a bit? Who might have had a stake in needing to shut them up about something?"

"I've wracked my brain, and I'm not closer to figuring it out than I was three weeks ago."

"Putting our heads together might help though. Tell me about Amanda. You said she embezzled money from you. How long had you known her? Did she grow up on the island?"

"Yeah, she grew up here. She'd worked for me for

about a month before we started dating. She made it clear she was interested, and I took the bait. I knew she loved nice things, but I was tired of being alone and easily swallowed the lie that she cared for me and not my bank account."

There was such cynicism in his voice that she nearly winced. "You sound pessimistic about romance."

He glanced at her. "Aren't you the same? Failure tends to do that to a person."

She decided not to answer that. Her own failures were better left unexamined. "When did you begin to suspect she wasn't all she seemed?"

"Not until the other accountant rubbed my face in what she'd done. She was good at deception. Even when I confronted her, I thought she would have a good explanation and would beg for forgiveness."

"She didn't?"

He shook his head. "She basically said she never loved me."

"Did she say why she took the money?" Wynne couldn't figure out why Amanda would have been so stupid. A month later and everything Simon had would have been half hers.

The expression of pain that flashed over Simon's face was quickly squelched. His knuckles turned white on the wheel. "I'd rather not talk about it," he said.

Wynne's cheeks stung as though she'd been slapped. "I see."

He sighed. "That didn't come out right." He glanced back at the other three crew members. "I'd rather talk when there's no chance of being overheard," he said softly. "How about dinner tonight?"

She studied his face for several long moments. "Is this a date?" She sucked in her breath as she waited for the answer. Her own temerity surprised her.

His eyes narrowed as he studied her face, then a hint of a smile tugged at his lips. "Yeah. You okay with that?"

"Maybe. It depends on if you're willing to let go of the past."

He turned his head and stared at her. "Are you?"

"I accepted, didn't I?"

He grinned. "It's like the blind leading the blind. We're both no geniuses at relationships. But maybe we can learn together."

The yearning expression in his eyes made her eyes prick with moisture. "Maybe," she said softly as they headed for the water.

By the time the day had ended, they'd found enough artifacts to convince the most skeptical scientist of the validity of their find. The storm that had shifted the sediment on the bottom had tossed up so much loot she couldn't believe it. Wynne nearly vibrated with excitement. She knew they had to keep it secret for now, but she longed to tell the world about the discovery.

But it was Simon's baby. It had been his vision, his commitment that had brought them to this place. His drive and determination. Once she'd thought him a little obsessed, and now she realized it had been conviction and not obsession.

The rest of the crew walked slowly off toward the parking lot, their steps dragging from the hard day's work. Wynne knew she should feel just as exhausted, but she was too wired to feel it.

Her stomach rumbled. "I heard that," Simon said. "I've got an idea." He opened the truck door for her then shut it behind her and pulled out his cell phone. She saw him talking as he walked around to his side of the vehicle.

"What was that all about?"

"You'll see." His smile was smug. "You deserve something nicer than Bob's Eats tonight."

"Surely you jest," she said in mock horror. "What could be better than greasy hamburgers?"

"How about lobster with garlic, mashed potatoes and steamed vegetables that are still at the edge of crispness. And follow it all up with a chocolate dessert that I can't even describe."

Her mouth dropped. "And just where are we going to find a meal like that on Eagle Island? Unless you got down and kissed our housekeeper's feet. Moxie might be able to whip up something like that. The chocolate dessert anyway."

"Beep, wrong answer." His grin widened as he turned onto the drive that led to the grassy airfield.

She lifted her brows as he stopped at the hangar. "What's going on?"

"We're flying into Marquette for dinner. There's a wonderful seafood restaurant on the water."

"But look at me," she protested. "I'm in wet jeans,

my hair looks like Medusa's, and I don't have a stitch of makeup left."

"You look beautiful to me," he said, his glance sliding sideways to linger on her face.

Heat traveled up her neck to her cheeks. "I can't go like this, Simon. I'll be the laughingstock of the town."

"Let me make one more call." He turned away and dialed his cell phone again.

She tried to listen, but the wind snatched his soft words away. It was sweet of him to want to treat her, but she would be mortified to go into a restaurant looking like this. She glanced at her watch. It was only five o'clock. Maybe he'd give her an hour to run home and get cleaned up.

He dropped his phone back into his pocket as a beat-up truck pulled up to the hangar. "There's our pilot."

"I've got to go home and get changed," she said firmly.

"It's all taken care of at the other end," he said. His fingers touched her elbow and guided her toward the runway.

She assumed they were headed for the small plane at the end of the runway, but instead Simon turned toward a helicopter to the right. "You're kidding, right?" She'd always wanted to ride in a helicopter.

"Nope." He helped her aboard.

She settled into the seat. "Simon, I need to change," she wailed.

"I told you—it's all taken care of. Let me spend a

little of my money in celebration. This is a big day—the biggest of my life so far."

"I thought the sheriff told you not to leave the island."

"He'll never know. Besides, I think he's figuring out that I'm not a murderer."

The "bird" took off, and they landed in Marquette less than thirty minutes later. Wynne was fascinated by the ride and the sound of the *whup-whup* of the rotors. The pilot ducked out of the helicopter and came around to open the door.

Simon helped her out and led her toward a coach limousine. Wynne felt she was in some kind of dream. Or nightmare might be closer to how she felt. She thought the limo driver was sneering as he opened the door.

"Go ahead, we'll wait out here while you change," Simon said.

"What?" Wynne nearly shrieked the words. She peeked into the coach.

"There's a shower in the bathroom. I called Becca and she said you wore a size two. There are three dresses to choose from and shoes in your size in the bathroom along with makeup." He shrugged apologetically. "I'm not sure the colors are right but you can try them."

"I can't believe this." She glared at him. "I warned you not to use the famous Lassiter charm on me." She folded her arms across her chest and willed herself not to cry. If he was expecting her to fall at his feet in admiration, he was going to wait a long time.

He scowled. "I know my money doesn't impress you, Wynne. But don't spoil my fun tonight. We had a great coup today. We can't announce it to the world yet, but we can celebrate. I couldn't have done it without you. Let me spoil you just a little."

She felt a stab of guilt. Maybe she had overreacted. There had been so much talk of how Amanda had been interested in his money, and she didn't want to be lumped into the same category with Simon's ex-fiancée. "Okay," she said after a long pause. "But don't try to turn my head after tonight."

"I'm not trying to do that." Simon's fingers touched her chin. "I want to thank you. Is that so wrong?"

Maybe not, but the touch of his fingers on her face was affecting her breathing. "I'll get changed," she said abruptly.

All she could do was pray for God to help her keep her heart intact. She bolted for the coach limo and slammed the door behind her. The bathroom had every luxury. She quickly ducked under the showerhead. Drying her hair with the hair dryer that was mounted on the wall, she wrapped it in an elegant French twist.

She opened the closet door and found three dresses hanging on the rod. The price tags had been removed, foiling her original plan to choose the cheapest one. Touching the fabric of each, she knew no expense had been spared on the dresses. Black shoes in a size four sat on the floor.

The red dress caught her eye. It had a boatneck collar and shimmered with a subtle shine. She slipped it over her head and turned to examine herself in the full-length mirror. She nearly didn't recognize the woman staring back at her.

Perfect. It clung in all the right places and turned at the knee in a becoming flip. She thrust her feet into the shoes and went out to meet Simon.

Her heart pounded as she opened the door to the outside. Would he think she looked nice? Her palms were sweaty. She took a deep breath and stepped down to the grass.

Simon turned to meet her. His mouth dropped, and he looked dazed. "W-Wynne?" he stammered.

"I love the dress, Simon. Thank you," she said, nearly breathless from the look on his face.

He stepped forward and touched her cheek. "All I can say is wow," he said softly. "Am I forgiven yet?"

"I'll think about it," she said as he tucked her hand into the crook of his elbow. "As long as you feed me lobster."

He escorted her back into the coach limo and sat her on the overstuffed leather sofa. "Something to drink?" he asked, turning toward the fully equipped bar.

"Sparkling water?"

"Got some right here." He poured it over ice and handed it to her, then grabbed a soda for himself before joining her on the sofa.

She wanted to press the cold glass against her hot face. Never had she been so aware of a man. She realized she was falling for him quite hopelessly. He was everything she'd ever wanted in a man—kind, strong, caring and, most importantly, a Christian. But his wealth bothered her. And she didn't want to give up her dreams of fame in her field. She'd have to travel to do it.

She sat stiffly, then Simon slipped his arm across the back of the sofa. She sagged against him as his bulk shifted her weight. She started to pull away, but his embrace pulled her against his side.

He dropped a kiss onto her head. "I like how you smell."

His breath stirred her hair, and her skin tingled where the warmth lingered. It was all she could do not to turn and wrap her arms around his neck. She curled her fingers into her palms and prayed for strength.

His fingers ran along the curve of her jaw and lingered at her earlobe. She shivered, a delicious sensation that stretched to her toes. His fingers trailed down to her chin and tilted her face up to meet his. When his lips found hers, she sank into his embrace.

Her heart hammered against her ribs and drowned out the warnings her mind tried to throw out.

She loved Simon. It was too late. She was lost—in over her head. And if the emotion in his kiss was any indication, he felt the same way.

He raised his head and smiled shakily as the coach stopped. Neon lights from the restaurant shone through the windows. "Let's go to dinner before I forget why we came."

"Good idea," she quavered.

He stood and helped her to her feet. His hand at her

waist felt like the softest touch of velvet, yet she knew he was tough and strong and protective.

All through dinner they stared into one another's eyes, and neither had much to say. Wynne knew the ground had shifted under her feet, and she could only hope Simon felt the same way.

NINETEEN

The house was dark when Simon got out of the truck. In his imagination, he saw Wynne waiting for him at home, then he dismissed the thought. Amanda had wanted this house, not him. He couldn't bring Wynne to a place another woman designed.

What was he thinking? He'd known Wynne Baxter for less than a month. How could he be thinking of marriage already? But he was. He'd recognized something in her that spoke to his soul in a way he'd never experienced. She completed him. He'd never thought of something like that. Always before, he'd analyzed the pros and cons of a woman as with a merger. Assets and liabilities, that's what he knew best. This wild emotion that made his palms go sweaty was outside his experience.

He suddenly became aware of a movement to his left and jerked around to meet the danger. His fists dropped when he recognized Sheriff Mitch Rooney.

"That's a good way to get clobbered, Rooney," he said. "Especially with everything that's been going on lately."

"We raised the yacht today," Rooney said, his voice deadpan and even.

"I thought you were going to have Wynne help you."

"We managed without her."

Rooney was acting weird, Simon thought. His hands dangled at his side as though he was too tired to raise them.

"Find anything?"

"Yeah." Rooney took a step closer. "A big hole blown in the underside."

Simon's attention sharpened. "Not caused by the shipwreck?"

"No, it was caused by an explosion from the inside. Murder." Rooney seemed to shake himself. "I think it's time you told me about the argument with Amanda."

"I told you it doesn't have anything to do with this case." Simon wanted to stride past the sheriff and gain the safety of the house. He stood his ground.

"That won't fly anymore, Simon. If I don't get a satisfactory answer, I'm going to have to haul you in for questioning. The judge won't want to be disturbed at this hour, so if you don't want to spend the night in jail, I suggest you start talking. And know I'm going to take your secretary in for questioning, too. You might as well tell me before she does."

He held out his hands. "Looks like you'll have to

take me downtown then." The clink of the handcuffs startled him, then the sheriff shoved him toward the squad car.

The moss and leaves under her feet seemed alive as Wynne strode through the forest. Blue spruce and hemlock snatched at her clothing as she followed the path to the folly. She'd forgotten all about this place until Becca had mentioned it last night. Her curiosity had gotten the best of her when she woke at daybreak, and she'd slipped out while everyone slept.

She needed to think. About Simon and her career—her entire future. It had once seemed so certain. Now she didn't know if she was right side up or upside down. She followed the twisting path toward the meadow.

Dawn had quickly yielded to the hot morning sunshine. She stepped from the shelter of the trees into the clearing and surveyed the ruins. The folly had been a favorite place for her and Becca to play when they were small. It was even more decrepit now. And unsafe. She'd best not investigate now, though it was fun to see it again.

She turned to go back to the house and almost knocked down an Ojibwa woman. About sixty, the woman's hair was still black and silky with faint wings of white at the temple. Dressed in a calico skirt and red peasant blouse, the buckskin vest she wore over her outfit was stained with berries and other juices Wynne couldn't identify.

"Sorry, I didn't see you." Wynne took a step back.

The woman didn't smile or acknowledge Wynne's apology. Her black eyes bored into Wynne's.

Wynne began to feel a sense of unease at the intensity of the woman's gaze. A crow gave a hoarse caw from the top of a sycamore tree, and the harshness raised the hair on the back of Wynne's neck.

"Can I help you?" she asked.

The woman took a step closer. "No good will come of disturbing the dead."

Wynne assumed the woman was talking about Jerry and Amanda. "You need to talk to the sheriff about that. I have nothing to do with it."

"The white men who came to these waters long ago were representatives of the Thunderbird. Let them rest in peace. You have no right to disturb their rest."

Wynne realized the woman somehow knew they'd found the remains of the Viking ship. "Who told you about the Viking ship?"

The woman's intent stare never wavered. "The Thunderbird will carry you off to feed her young if you continue to disturb the remains. This will be your only warning. Stop before it's too late." The woman turned and disappeared into the woods before Wynne could form an answer.

Wynne stared after her. She wished people could understand how important archaeological discovery was. Everywhere she went, people objected for some reason or another. This was no different.

In spite of telling herself these were the same objections she'd encountered countless times before, a chill raced down her spine. There had been so much menace in the matter-of-fact way the woman had uttered her warning. Ridiculous.

She refused to allow the woman's ramblings to disturb this time alone. A large rock sat in the sunshine, and she settled herself on it. "God, what am I supposed to do?"

She wished He'd give her a sign, some indication of what path to follow. If she followed her heart, she'd give up her dream. If she followed her dream, her heart would be broken. It was a no-win situation. Only God could figure it out. After fifteen minutes, she decided He wasn't speaking.

Wynne rose and hurried back the way she'd come. Maybe Max or Becca would have some idea of who the woman was she'd run into. She burst out of the trees and into the backyard of Windigo Manor. She barreled into Max's chest.

He gripped her by the shoulders and steadied her. "Whoa, where's the fire?"

"Sorry," she panted. "There was a woman back there." Aware she was babbling, she stopped and took a deep, calming breath. "Someone knows we've found the Viking boat." She quickly told him what the Ojibwa woman had said.

"This isn't good. If she knows, the word will get out. If everyone knows, Mike Wilson will likely show up next, and we'll have a fight on our hands."

"We'd better get out to the site right away," Wynne

agreed. "Let me change into my suit. You call Simon." She rushed upstairs and changed into her swimsuit, then pulled shorts and a tank top over it.

As she stepped into the living room, her gaze wandered to the TV where the anchorman was giving the weather forecast. She listened, her frown deepening. She and Becca looked at one another.

"The big storm will be here in two days," Becca said.

"We have to work fast," she agreed. "The storm could bury the remains too deep to retrieve. The woman said the Thunderbird didn't like it. With this storm blowing in, she would say the Thunderbird was determined to thwart our efforts."

Becca looked confused. "What woman?"

Wynne told her about the Ojibwa woman. A name on the television caught their attention. She turned and listened then looked at her sister. "Simon's been arrested?" she said in shock. "But how can that be?"

"You'd better get to the jail," Becca said. "Max will take you. I'll get him." She rushed from the room and left Wynne staring at the television.

Max burst into the room followed by Becca and Gram. Gram was wringing her hands. "We have to do something, Max. We know Simon is no murderer."

"I know, Gram. We'll get him out," he said grimly. "Will you watch the kids? I think Wynne might like Becca along."

"Of course," Gram said. She took the baby from Becca.

Wynne followed Max and Becca to his truck. She stared out the window as Max barreled down the road to town. What possible evidence could the sheriff have that would have caused him to arrest Simon? Could she have been wrong about Simon?"

"I see that look on your face," Becca said. "Don't go there. Simon isn't guilty. Have a little faith in him, Wynne. I think you love him. I've seen it in your eyes the last few days. But love is nothing without trust. This is one of those times you have to step out on faith."

"I'm trying," she said weakly. "How do I get past my doubts?"

"I think you have to listen, Wynne. Trust the Spirit of God who reveals truth to you. I think sometimes you run things over too much in your mind without asking for God to reveal truth to your heart. Listen for a change and stop the inner dialogue."

Wynne's spirit smote her. Becca was right. She needed to shut up and listen. She listened to everyone else, but tended to tune out God. "Okay," she said meekly. She leaned her head back against the headrest. Quieting her heart, she listened for the still, small voice inside. The voice she often shouted to silence with her thoughts.

When she opened her eyes, she knew God had answered. All it had taken was for her to shut up long enough for His words to get through. She smiled at Max. "Let's go get Simon out of jail."

"Attagirl," he said. He maneuvered the truck through the pedestrians and parked in front of the jail.

Wynne was out almost before the truck had rolled to a stop. She took the sidewalk at a dead run and burst into the sheriff's office with Max and Becca on her heels.

The woman behind the counter jumped defensively when Wynne banged her fist on the counter. "I want to see Simon Lassiter," Wynne said.

"Just a minute, I'll get the sheriff," the woman said. She rose and hurried down the hall. It was nearly five minutes later before she returned. "Sheriff Rooney will be here in a few minutes. He was out late last night and isn't in the office yet."

"I'll wait." Wynne went to the row of chairs along the back wall. Max and Becca joined her. She'd flipped through a hunting magazine when Rooney finally showed up.

His uniform was a bit rumpled, and there were dark circles under his eyes. Wariness crept into his face when he saw the three of them. "Follow me," he barked. He strode down the hall to the last office on the right. "Have a seat. I'd offer you coffee but it's yesterday's and it was lousy then." He dropped into the cracked leather chair behind the desk.

"I want to see Simon," Wynne began.

"I figured you weren't here to shoot the breeze with me," Rooney sighed. "I'll let you see him, but I need you to get him to talk to me. He's hiding something. And until I know what it is, my gut tells me it has something to do with the murders."

"Murders!" Wynne exclaimed at the same time as Max and Becca.

"Yep. An explosion sank the yacht. It was no accident."

Wynne shuddered. Though she knew it had to have been murder with all the things that had been happening, she'd still hoped there was some other explanation. "Let me talk to Simon," she said slowly.

"Follow me." Rooney stood and took keys from his desk drawer then led her to the confinement area.

The hall stank of despair. Wynne wanted to run for the sunshine, but she wanted Simon more than she wanted air.

"Wynne!"

She heard Simon call her name just ahead to the left. She bolted past Rooney and reached the cell before he did. She thrust her fingers through the bars and touched his. He looked tired and drawn, but the light in his eyes warmed her.

"You shouldn't be here," he said. He bent down and kissed her fingertips.

She wanted to tear down the bars and free him with her bare hands. She turned to Rooney. "Let him out. You have no cause to keep him."

"Hold your horses," he grumbled. He unlocked the cell and swung open the door. "You got fifteen minutes."

Wynne paid no attention. She barreled into the cell and threw herself into Simon's arms. He caught her and kissed her then buried his face in her hair.

"What are you doing here?" he whispered.

"What's happened? How could he arrest you?" she demanded.

"He can't keep me. He has no evidence."

She pulled back and looked up into his face. "He says you're hiding something. Are you?"

"He wants to know about the argument. I can't tell him. He'll throw away the key and I'll never get out of here."

Wynne's gaze searched his face. "I learned something today. It's about faith and trust and truth. God is truth, and He never steers us wrong. If we listen to Him, He guides us into what's true and right and good."

His hands dropped from her shoulders. He slumped. "You want me to tell him?"

She regarded him steadily. "Yes. Let's both trust God and step out in faith."

He straightened his shoulders. "Okay. But I want you there."

"I wouldn't be anywhere else."

TWENTY

Simon sat in Rooney's office. Wynne sat beside him and held his hand. Becca and Max were waiting in the reception area. Simon returned the pressure of Wynne's fingers. His pulse throbbed.

Rooney pushed a mini tape deck forward. "Okay if I turn this on?"

"I guess." Simon's mouth was dry. "Can I have some water?"

"I'll get it." Wynne jumped up and went to the water cooler and filled two paper cups.

Simon took a gulp and the cool water cleared his jumbled thoughts. He drew in a deep breath. "Okay, you wanted to know what the argument was about. You already know I found out she was embezzling from me. The rest of it is just a continuation of the sordid mess. Amanda told me she had taken the money for Jerry to invest in the business. That he'd promised her a huge return on her money if she could get him a hundred thousand dollars." He didn't dare look at Wynne. He didn't want to see disappointment in her eyes.

"And?" Rooney prompted.

"And if she could make enough money, she wouldn't need me," Simon finished. "She was using me for my money. She'd never loved me. I was just her latest cash cow."

"And that angered you, I'm sure. How did you blow the hole in the boat?"

"I didn't. She begged me to cover her embezzlement or she'd implicate me in the crime as well."

"Blackmail." Rooney's expression was deadpan.

"Not really. I wasn't afraid of her. I told her I'd cover for her, but our engagement was off. She told me to meet her at lunch and she'd give me my money back—that she'd get it back from Jerry. I went to meet her, but she never showed. I heard she'd gone off on the boat with her suitcase, and I knew she'd scammed me. She had no intention of paying back the money."

A weight felt as if it had lifted from Simon's shoulders. He squeezed Wynne's fingers again. She was right. It felt good to get it all out in the open. It sounded bad, but hiding it had been worse. He dared a glance at her and smiled at the trust he saw in her eyes. His revelation hadn't shattered her faith in him.

"That's it?" Rooney sounded disgusted.

"Yeah."

Rooney heaved an exasperated sigh. "Get out of here. I've already heard most of this."

* * *

Max drove back to Windigo Manor while Wynne told Max and Becca what had happened. She kept glancing at Simon, but he sat with his eyes closed and his head on the headrest. He must have had a rough night. He kept possession of her hand though.

Once they reached Windigo Manor, Simon pulled her to one side. "Let's go check on our Viking treasure," he said. "What if my being arrested allowed someone to steal it?"

"I'm sure it's fine," she said soothingly. "But sure, we can go. Do you need to call the others?"

"I guess we could use some backup." He dragged his cell phone out and called Joe and Bjorn. "Bjorn is busy but Joe can come."

As they hurried out to the boat dock, Simon took her hand in a natural way that caught her by surprise. The warm clasp of his fingers around hers sent a rush of heat to her cheeks. She clung to his hand as they hurried along the uneven ground to the waiting boat. Simon stepped aboard then helped her hop onto the deck. Her sandal snagged on something, and she lost her balance and fell against him.

He caught her against his chest. She could hear the way the thud of his heart sped up under her ear. The masculine scent of him dried her mouth. And she had the most insane urge to slide her arms around his neck and lift her face up to meet his. What would he do if she did that? Run the other way, most likely, though she knew he wasn't immune to her. Still, was it the same depth of feeling that raged in her own heart?

While all the thoughts and impressions raced through her head, she realized Simon was still holding her, and she was still liking it. She looked up into his eyes. The expression in his face made it impossible to move. His right hand slid up her arm, clear up to her cheek. He rubbed his thumb over her cheekbone.

"You have the most expressive face I've ever seen," he murmured. "I'm not going to hurt you, Wynne."

"I'm trying to trust in that area, too," she croaked. She couldn't have moved away if her life depended on it.

"You're different from every other woman I've ever met. Let your heart tell you the truth of this." His left arm cinched her more tightly against his chest, and his lips came down to meet hers.

A myriad of emotions raced through her—elation, desire, and fear all vied for control. She wrapped her arms around his neck and lost herself in the warmth of his lips. She couldn't think, could barely breathe.

Caution screamed for her attention, and she finally dragged her mouth from his.

He slowly opened his eyes. "Wow, again," he said. "Is it going to be that way every time I kiss you?"

"I don't know." She bit her trembling lower lip. "I think we'd better stick to business."

"I'm not so sure about that," he said softly. His eyes crinkled up at the corners as the tenderness in his eyes grew.

Wynne knew she had to move or she would be lost in that gaze. She stepped back and dropped her arms from around him. "We'd better get out there. We don't have long."

"This isn't over," Simon said. "When we have time, we're going to talk about us."

"There is no us," Wynne said. But she knew it was a feeble excuse.

"Maybe not yet," was all Simon said as he helped her aboard the boat.

Her heart resumed its normal rhythm by the time Joe joined them and they cast off. She hardly dared look at Simon as they rode the waves to the coordinates. They suited up and went overboard. The shock of cold water helped get her thoughts organized again. They would have time to sort this out later.

Wynne sank down to the bottom of the lake. Nothing appeared to have been disturbed. She gave Simon the thumbs-up, and he nodded, his smile lifting behind his mask. They worked for two hours then headed back to the boat.

Rising to the sunshine, Wynne was ready for a break. She wanted time to examine what had happened the last few days. She felt like her life was a fast steamer on a track to the unknown, and she didn't know if she should jump ship or not.

Simon could barely keep his thoughts on the job at hand, and that fact was an indication of how powerful his feelings for Wynne had developed. The Viking ship had obsessed him for years, but what he felt when he kissed Wynne had been a firestorm of emotion he'd never experienced. Diving in the cold water cleared his head, but it didn't clear the yearning he felt to have Wynne in his arms again.

By the end of the day, they had gathered Viking jewelry, combs, knives and beads. Their treasure had been cataloged and locked away. "I'm done working for the day. How about some fun?"

Wynne's concentrated frown smoothed, and she looked up at him from where she crouched, sifting the last pail of muck from the bottom of the lake. "What did you have in mind?"

"How about a picnic on Gull Island?"

A delighted smile lifted her lips. "I've been wanting to get out there and go bird-watching. Becca says she's seen a snowy egret there."

"Oh, yeah, I've seen all kinds of birds out there. There's a nice beach, too. Not that we want to get back in the water."

"I don't know, I could work on my tan a bit. We don't get much sun being covered with a dry suit and underwater all day."

Simon's gaze lingered on her face. She had a light tan, and the sunshine had popped out a sprinkling of freckles across her nose.

Color spread over her cheeks at his perusal. "I wish you'd stop looking at me like that," she murmured.

"Like what?" He was getting a kick out of disconcerting her.

"You know perfectly well what I mean." She looked away. "What about food for this picnic?"

"We'll drop Joe off at the dock, then stop at the café and get fried chicken and coleslaw. They've also got a sinfully rich chocolate brownie."

"Now you're talking my language."

He loved to watch the way her face changed expression. There were so many facets of her personality that drew him. She didn't hide behind a mask like so many women. She put herself out there for a friend to accept or reject, and Simon found himself embracing that transparency. It was a refreshing change.

They stopped by the café and loaded up on food, then got back on board and headed out to Gull Island. Wynne sat in the bow with the wind whipping her long black hair back from her face.

The island came into view, and he guided the boat to the sheltered inlet, then dropped anchor. He handed Wynne the food. "You carry the food, and I'll carry you."

Her eyebrows winged up. "I don't need to be carried."

"Have you ever been here before?" He grimaced. "It's mucky here and the lily pads will try to swallow you whole." He jumped into the water. "Come here and quit arguing."

A smile eased her frown. "Chivalry isn't dead, huh?" Holding the sack of food, she slipped her arms around his neck and leaned into his chest.

He slid his arm under her knees and lifted her from

the boat. The mud sucked at his bare feet, and he staggered when a rogue wave struck him in the back. A mat of lily pads wrapped itself around his knees, and he struggled to free himself.

Wynne was shaking, and he looked into her face. She was struggling to smother her laughter, but it burst out when their gazes connected. "Some knight you are. You're trapped, aren't you?"

"Of course not." He jerked on his right foot, but it held fast in the mud. He tried the other foot. No luck. "Okay, maybe I am stuck." If it weren't for the smile on her face, he might have been embarrassed, but the delight in her eyes made a deep rumble of laughter erupt from his chest.

"You're enjoying this too much. Maybe I should let the lily pads have you." He acted like he was going to toss her into the waves, and she clutched him tighter.

"If I go down, so do you," she warned. The sunlight glinted in her hair and lit her face.

"I'm convinced." He tried to pull on his foot again. "Any ideas how we get out of this? I can see the headlines now—Famous Marine Archaeologist Found Floating Among The Lily Pads."

She giggled again, and he wasn't sure he'd ever heard someone laugh with such delight and abandon. He could spend a lifetime listening to her laughter.

The realization tightened his face, and his smile died. His gaze searched her face and lingered on her lips.

The merry light in her eyes faded, and she looked up at him with a transparent expression.

Simon knew he was treading on dangerous ground, but he couldn't resist the way she caught her lower lip in her white teeth and gazed at him with such yearning. He bent his head and his lips found hers. Her warm breath whispered across his face, and he inhaled the scent of her—the hint of mint on her breath, the underlying aroma of fresh lake water and herbal scent in her hair. Her lips were warm and yielding under his, and she kissed him back.

When he pulled away, they were both breathless.

"I don't think that's going to get us free from the lily pads," Wynne whispered.

"Maybe not, but it sure makes our predicament more fun." He tried to smile, but couldn't carry it off.

He loved Wynne Baxter, and he wasn't quite sure what he was going to do about it.

TWENTY-ONE

"So, my dear, what are you going to do to get us out of this predicament?" Wynne tightened her grip on Simon's neck. She was in no hurry for him to put her down.

"I'm not sure. Got any ideas?" He tugged at his foot again then shrugged.

"You'd better put me down," she said. "Float back into the water and let your legs come up."

"I'm not sure I like that answer," he said. "We'll both be soaked."

"We've got dry clothes on the boat. I'll get them while you get loose."

He lowered her into the water, and the shock of cold cleared her head. What had she been thinking? The deeper she got in with Simon, the more the thought of her new project in Australia failed to excite her. She had signed a contract, and she had to go.

She flayed through the water and clambered aboard

the boat, then wrapped dry clothes for both of them in plastic. Holding the plastic package over her head, she waded to shore. Simon had extricated himself and was busy gathering wood for a fire on the sand.

"I'll get the food," she said, wading back to the boat. The waves struck her as they rolled toward the beach, and she staggered at their cold slap. Arming herself with the picnic basket, she trudged back to shore.

"I'm going to get changed," she told him. "You stay here."

"Aye, aye, captain," he said, saluting.

She trotted down the path to a small lean-to that had been on the island for as long as she could remember. She ducked inside and quickly changed her clothes. Once she was warm and dry, she hurried back to the beach and found a fire sputtering on the wet wood Simon had found.

She held her hands over the flames. "Got any marshmallows?"

"Nary a one. Sorry. Want a blanket?" He'd changed while she was gone as well.

She was still cold. "You have one?"

"Your wish is my command." He dug in the picnic basket and brought out a cotton blanket. "It's not heavy but it's warm."

"Anything will help," she said as he dropped it around her shoulders. He'd pulled logs around the fire, and she settled down on one. "I'm famished. Did you happen to call and tell my family I'd be late? I meant to do that when we stopped for the food."

"I didn't think about it." He frowned. "We can't call now, either. Gull Island is in a dead spot and the cell phone doesn't work. Want me to take the boat out to a spot where it works and call them?"

"No, no, it's fine. We won't be that late." She opened the picnic basket. "Let's chow down on some chicken before it gets cold."

Before Simon could answer her, she saw a movement from the corner of her eye. She stood and waved her arms. "Hey, get away from there!" Their boat was being pulled away from shore by a small boat.

The figure clad in dark clothing was too far away to see his face. Simon ran to the edge of the water and waded in, then dove into the waves to try to catch hold of the boat. Wynne knew it was a lost cause. The small boat's engine fired and both boats moved off quickly.

Simon returned to shore. "We're stuck," he said. "No one knows we're here."

Wynne had already thought of that. "What are we going to do?"

"I'm not sure." He sneezed and began to shiver.

"Here, take this blanket." She wrapped it around him. "Your other clothes are still soaking wet, too. Let me see if I can get them dry." She went to the fire and shoved some rocks as close to the blaze as she could. She draped Simon's wet clothes on the rocks.

"That's going to take a while," Simon said. "The storm will be here by morning. We need to find a way off before then."

Wynne nodded. "Let's explore the island and see what's here."

"There used to be an old canoe on the leeward side of the island. Maybe it's still there." Simon took her hand, and they walked along the sand to the other side of the tiny island.

"Who is doing this, Simon?" Wynne tightened her grip on his hand. "I'm getting scared. And what was the purpose of this?"

He stopped on the sand and pulled her close. "I don't want to scare you more but in a big storm, a surge can flood the island. I'd say it's an attempt to kill us."

"But why?" she asked, her voice muffled against his wet chest. She shivered, not so much from Simon's cold clothing but from the bleak situation.

"I've been trying to think of that, too. It could be Wilson. He might want the Viking site. It's worth more than money—it's prestige. Or maybe it's Alan and he's out for revenge."

"An old girlfriend of Jerry's?" Wynne suggested.

"But why? Jerry is dead. So is Amanda. What would she gain by killing us?"

Wynne pulled away and rubbed the moisture from her cheek. "I have no idea. Have you offended any old girlfriends? Maybe she thought she was killing you when she sank the yacht, and when she found out she got the wrong man, she's trying again."

"It's a stretch, even if I had wounded a woman, which I haven't." He took her hand again, and they continued to march around the island.

"There it is," Wynne said, pointing to the old canoe. "Is it sound?"

Simon knelt and rolled it over. He inspected the sides and bottom. "Looks like it. But in these high waves, it's going to be dangerous to try to paddle it to Eagle Island. I want you to stay here until I send back help."

"No way." Wynne shook her head. "I'm going with you. If we don't make it, at least we'll be together." She stopped short, aware of what she'd just admitted if he had the insight to hear.

His gaze caught hers, and she saw the same awareness in his eyes. He cupped her face in his hands. His lips came down on hers. The promise in his kiss gave her hope and courage.

"We're going to make it," he said, looking deep into her eyes. "I know it's quick, but I love you, Wynne. I guess this is the first time I've ever really felt this way."

"I love you, too," she whispered. She glanced at the sky. "Now let's get out of here."

Simon couldn't see any holes in the canoe, but it wasn't the best looking craft he'd ever seen. There was only one paddle, and it was chipped and battered. He had to wonder if it would make it without breaking on the high surf. He found a split branch that was sort of flat on one end and handed it to Wynne.

"You can try to steer us with that," he told her. Looking at her, he knew he had to find a way to get them both out of this mess. He should have told someone where they were going. This was his fault. If he'd just slowed down and thought this through.

The clouds hung low in the sky, and a stiff wind blew from the north. Simon shivered in his still wet clothes. It was hard to believe it was summer with the cold chill in the air, but the weather on Lake Superior was capricious.

He thought about changing his clothes again. The ones by the fire might be slightly less wet than what he wore, but he dismissed the idea. He'd be drenched again in minutes so there was no use in wasting the time.

He and Wynne dragged the canoe to the water. "Get in," he told her. He glanced at his watch. Five o'clock. There were a few hours of daylight left, but they'd need to move fast from the look of the sky.

Wynne hopped into the boat, and he shoved it along the last bit of sand until it floated freely in the waves. He clambered over the side, nearly tipping it before they were even offshore.

Wynne grabbed the sides of the canoe and hung on. "Whoa!"

Simon steadied the canoe with the paddle. "We're okay." He stood and pushed the paddle into the sand under the water, then sat back down and began to paddle in the direction of Eagle Island.

"How long do you think it will take us to get there?" Wynne asked. From the bow of the boat, she thrust the branch in the water and helped steady it.

"A couple of hours probably." He didn't add "if the

winds cooperate." He didn't have to. Wynne knew as well as he did that the situation was desperate.

Away from the island, the winds battered them and their small craft. Wynne's hair soon came loose from its braid and blew around her head. She kept thrusting it out of her face, and Simon wished he had a rubber band for her.

He knew she had to be as cold as he was. Probably colder. "Take the blanket," he yelled. He thrust it toward her, and she took it. It wouldn't help much, he knew. It was soaking wet. But at least it would be another layer.

Blisters rose on his hands as he doggedly fought the waves. "Looks like the Thunderbird is out today!" he shouted above the roar of the wind.

"I've been praying," Wynne called back. Her cheeks were pale, and her eyelashes were spiky from the constant spray in her face.

The sky darkened even more. Thunder began to rumble in the distance, then grew closer as streaks of lightning flashed across the sky.

Wynne flinched and hunkered down onto the floor of the canoe. "We're sitting ducks out here," she hollered. "I hate lightning."

"I didn't think you were afraid of anything." He grinned at her. His arms felt like they were going to fall off. There was still no sign of lights along the shore of Eagle Island. With the sun obscured, he wasn't positive they were even going in the right direction.

"Are we lost?" Wynne looked back at him.

"I hope not," he told her. He continued to doggedly paddle in what he hoped was the right direction.

"There," Wynne said suddenly. "I see lights." She pointed.

The rain began to fall, and Simon squinted through the curtain of moisture covering the landscape. "I see Turtle Town." He recognized the strip of neon lights that glared through the darkening clouds.

A rogue wave came out of nowhere and slammed into the canoe, nearly tipping them both into the waves that were taking on monstrous proportions. He fought to keep the canoe steady.

He heard Wynne scream and looked up to see a towering wave heading toward them. "Hang on!" he shouted. The wave slammed into the small craft. He swallowed water, then he was tumbling in the water, not sure which way was up and which was down. The black waves tossed him around and he could see nothing.

Wynne, he thought, his arms flailing. They might have had such a wonderful life together. It was all going to end here just a half mile from safety.

Wynne clung to the side of the upended canoe and scanned the rolling waves for Simon's head. Where was he? He'd disappeared when the giant wave had swamped the boat. She couldn't feel her fingers at all, though she knew she was still holding to the boat. She prayed with what little thoughts she could gather as she tried to stay conscious.

She saw something off to her left. “Simon!” She reached out toward his dark head bobbing in the waves. He was facedown. *Please, Lord, don’t let him be dead.* She released her hold on the canoe and managed to snag his shirt. She rolled him over. “Simon, wake up.” Her voice sounded was so weak it was barely above a whisper, but he must have heard because his lashes fluttered, and he coughed.

Waves kept rolling over their heads. She was so cold. “We’re almost to shore,” she urged him. “Come on, fight.”

He nodded and they began to swim for the shore. The lights seemed just out of reach. Wynne couldn’t feel her limbs or even her face anymore. Moving sent blood pumping through her head though, and her thoughts sharpened.

They could make it. She felt an inner voice urging her on. They wouldn’t give up so close to safety. Conscious of Simon struggling beside her, she focused on one kick after the other. Going through the motions. Her muscles screamed for rest, crowding out all other sensations: the cold, the howling wind, the water slapping her in the face.

Then her knees scraped sand. Another wave caught her and tossed her against some rocks. Her chin struck something hard, and she saw stars. The strength ran out of her arms and she sank then came up sputtering.

Simon had gained his feet. He grasped her hand and hauled her up against him. “I’ve got you now,” he muttered against her hair.

She sagged against him. He was trembling as much as she was. "I can't believe we made it," she whispered.

"I prayed with what little focus I could find," he said.

"Me, too." She wrapped her arms around his waist as the rain continued to pelt them.

"Let's get inside where we can get dry and warm." He led her toward the café. Bob's Eats looked as welcome as a bowl of hot chili on a winter night. The blast of warm air that hit them as they entered the restaurant enveloped Wynne like a blanket.

"I've lost my cell phone or I'd call your family," Simon told her. "I'd better find a pay phone."

She caught at his hand. "Don't leave me yet," she said. "I still can't believe we're alive. I just want to look at you."

He smiled wearily and draped his arm around her shoulders. They went to a back table.

Rhonda was working tonight. Her mouth dropped in shock. "What's happened to you? Here, have some coffee." She poured out two cups of coffee. "Who should I call for you?"

"Call the sheriff for one," Simon said. "Then if you'll bring me the phone, I'll call Wynne's family."

"Be right back." Rhonda hurried off toward the kitchen.

Wynne wrapped her hands around the hot cup. She wished she could dive in and have her whole body feel as warm as her hands. She took a sip and shuddered as the warm liquid made its way down her throat. She pressed the cup to her cold cheek.

Her gaze locked with Simon's. He'd said he loved her before they left the island. Did he mean it or was it just nerves talking? He regarded her steadily then reached across the table and took her hand.

"When this is all over, we need to talk. I think you'll agree there is an 'us' after all."

Welcome heat flooded her face. "I hope so." She felt suddenly shy. On the island when it had seemed there might not even be tomorrow, it had been easier to contemplate a future. Now the reasons she'd told herself that stood in the way crowded back for attention.

TWENTY-TWO

Sheriff Rooney put his pad and pen away. "I'll see if the Coast Guard can find your boat. You sure seem prone to losing it these days."

"We didn't lose it," Simon said testily. "Someone seems bent on drowning us. Why can't you figure out who is doing this?"

"You've seen this mysterious person and you still can't identify who it is," the sheriff pointed out.

Simon conceded, "I'm just tired of this."

Brian burst through the door. "I just heard what happened," he panted. "Are you both okay?"

"We're fine." Simon rubbed his head.

"Did you see who did this? I heard you were deliberately stranded."

"Yeah, we were. But God brought us through." Simon still couldn't believe it. They should have been dead at the bottom of the lake.

"The storm seems to be dying," Rooney said. "I'll see what we can do about finding your boat."

"It's not even mine," Simon said. "I borrowed it."

Rooney winced. "Maybe we'll find it." He didn't sound optimistic.

"What about tomorrow?" Brian asked. "We were going to go back to the Viking site."

"If it's not been covered up with silt." Simon felt as morose as he sounded. His body ached, and he fought the heavy droop of his lids. "We don't have a boat."

"Or a crew," Brian added. "Joe and Bjorn told me they were taking the day off and going to the mainland."

"Great, just great. Guess we're all taking a break."

Brian hesitated. "Maybe not. I've got a boat ready to launch, and the owner isn't taking possession for another few days. The three of us could go out. I can't be gone all day, but we could hit it in the afternoon."

"Perfect. That will give the silt and mud time to settle, and we'll see how much damage the storm caused."

"And we can sleep in," Wynne put in.

"There's that, too," Simon agreed. "I feel like I could sleep for a week."

Wynne yawned. "Me, too."

"I'll take you home," Brian said. "You look beat."

"I'll take her," Simon put in quickly.

Brian raised his eyebrows and grinned. "You're the boss."

Simon went toward the door. "I'll be back with the truck. Don't go anywhere." By the time he got back with his truck, Brian and the sheriff had left. Wynne was watching from the plate glass window, and she hurried out to hop in the passenger side.

"We never did get to eat our dinner," she said suddenly.

"I'm too tired to be hungry." Her stomach rumbled, and he laughed. "I guess you're not. Moxie will feed you though."

"Yeah." Her face brightened and he knew she was thinking about the welcome she would get when she arrived at Windigo Manor. He envied that type of family connection.

He dared hope he was going to be part of it one day. "Wynne," he began. He choked back the words when he saw that her eyes were closed. "Never mind," he whispered. "It can wait."

The tapping wouldn't go away. "Wynne, time to get up."

Wynne groaned and dragged the pillow over her head at the sound of Becca's voice. "Go away. Nobody lives here anymore."

The knocking just intensified. "I know you're in there. You've got a phone call."

Simon. "I'm up," she called. Wynne threw the covers back and snatched at the phone. "Hello," she said breathlessly.

"I hope I didn't awaken you."

Her heart fell. It was Gordon Masters, her boss on the upcoming project in Australia. "No, it's fine, Gordon. I was just out a little late last night." Late didn't begin to cover it. If a truck had run over her, she wouldn't have felt any worse.

"I just wanted to finalize our plans. I need you here a little earlier than we'd initially planned. Can you be here next week?"

"Next week! That's nearly a month early."

"I know, but our permit has come through, and I'm eager to get to work. E-mail me your travel arrangements and I'll have someone pick you up at the airport when you arrive."

In a mental fog, Wynne wrote down the information he rattled off and hung up. Next week. Her stomach plunged. She would have to leave Simon. She got up and moved to the bathroom. Her dark eyes looked stark in her white face, and her hair was a fright. Tangled and gnarled, it looked as bad as she'd ever seen it.

She turned on the shower and hopped in, letting the hot water ease the pain from her body. It was all she could to do hobble around and get ready. Her arms ached when she raised them to braid her hair, and she could barely stand upright.

She had to talk to Simon. Her lungs squeezed at the thought. She still didn't know what she would say. It had seemed so easy at Gull Island yesterday. Her thoughts were as tangled as her hair.

Still moving slowly, she dressed in jeans and went downstairs. Yesterday's storm left a freshness in the air, and she sniffed appreciatively. The house felt empty and silent. Where was everyone? She glanced at her watch. Eleven o'clock. Molly had a softball game.

She wandered into the kitchen and snagged an apple from the refrigerator, then headed out to the verandah. Munching her apple, she watched some sparrows flit along the flagstone as they scavenged for crumbs. She had to face this and decide what to do before she saw Simon.

What did she really want to do with her life? Shaking her head slightly, she stood and tossed the apple core to the birds, then headed toward the dock. Simon had said he'd pick her up at eleven-thirty, and it was nearly that now.

Walking down the slope, she heard the sound of an approaching boat coming toward the Manor's dock. Simon waved from the deck. She lifted her hand in greeting and watched the wind ruffle his hair.

She couldn't imagine leaving him, couldn't fathom not seeing him every day. Her heart ached as much as her body did. What could she do?

"I wasn't sure you'd be out of bed yet," he said, his smile widening as she stepped aboard the boat. "I called an hour ago, and Becca said you were still asleep."

"She should have woken me sooner." Her fingers curled around his, and he didn't relinquish her hand even though she was safely aboard the boat. He rubbed his thumb over the palm of her right hand, and shivers ran up her hand.

"I told her to let you sleep. I could have gone out without you today. Not that I wanted to though." His smile was tender.

She looked away. How could she tell him she was

leaving when he looked at her like that? "Nice boat," she said, directing her gaze to Brian.

He preened. "Yeah, it's a beauty. She took me months to design. I think our customer is going to be really happy."

"You've sure got some innovative ideas. I'm surprised the business hasn't really taken off."

"It's going to," Simon put in. "With some more capital invested, we'll spend some money on publicity." He stopped and clapped his left hand to his forehead. "I'm an idiot. I bought some replacement sieves but left them at the boatyard."

"We can run by and get them," Brian said, turning the wheel of the boat.

Simon tugged at Wynne's hand and led her out to the chair on the bow. There was only one. He sat in it and pulled her down on his lap. He rested his chin on the top of her head.

"I'm squishing you," she protested.

"You're no bigger than a mosquito," he said, his arms settling around her waist. "Besides, we can talk like this and not be overheard. I could hardly sleep last night for making plans."

He sounded happy and smug. Wynne hated the thought of breaking his bubble of happiness. "Simon," she began.

"Mmm." His lips sent a burst of warmth into her hair.

She might as well blurt it out and get it over with. "I got a call this morning. I'm supposed to go to Australia next week."

His fingers tightened on her waist, then he pulled his head back from her hair. "Wait...I don't understand. You mean you're just going to up and go after telling me you love me?"

"I signed a contract," she began.

"I realize that, but don't you think you should have told him you needed to discuss it with me first?"

"I *am* discussing it with you," she reminded him. "Besides, what is there to say? You know what my profession is."

He began to smile. "I wanted it to be a surprise, but I guess I'd better tell you. I want to buy a boat, one that will go anywhere in any seas. Like Jacques Cousteau. We can get a crew together and do our own dig."

Is that what his profession of love had meant? He hadn't said another word about it, and he hadn't asked her to marry him, either. She swallowed the lump in her throat. "I see," she said slowly.

His smile faded. "I'm going about this all wrong," he muttered. He tipped her head to the side and looked deeply into her eyes. "I want to marry you, Wynne. We can travel the world together, discover exciting things. I love you."

There. He'd finally spoken the words she'd longed to hear, but they felt flat somehow. Maybe it was just her fatigue. Seated on his lap with his breath in her face, she knew she loved him. But how much did he love her? Was it because she shared his love of history, and the water, or did he love her for herself?

And what about children? What about establishing

a home together? She didn't know how it would all work together. It all suddenly seemed overwhelming to her. "I still have a contract."

"I can pay to break it."

"I'd hate to leave Gordon in the lurch."

"But you'd willingly leave me." His voice was flat, and his body turned rigid.

"You're putting words in my mouth," she protested. "I have obligations. I can't just ignore them."

"Can't or won't?"

"Simon, be reasonable," she pleaded. She put her hands on the sides of his head and forced him to look at her when he tried to look away. "I love you. You know I do."

"Do I? Or are you like the rest and just interested in my money?" His voice grew louder.

"If it were your money I was after, I'd gladly take you up on your offer of a boat and complete funding," she reminded him. He scowled, and she smoothed the wrinkles on his forehead. "Don't yell at me, okay?" she whispered.

His face cleared. "I wasn't yelling. We were discussing it."

She pinched his lips together. "Say 'I'm sorry.' Come on, it isn't so hard. Say it!"

"I said I wasn't yelling." His lips began to turn up.

"Why is it men have such a hard time actually saying 'I'm sorry?' You're a big boy. You can admit you were wrong."

"Hang on, there. You're going too far now." He was

laughing now, his eyes crinkling at the corners. He stared into her eyes. "Is this the way it's always going to be? I'm going to be cajoled into admitting culpability when I'm innocent?"

She suddenly realized it was going to be all right. Their respect for one another and their humor would carry them when things got rough. "Probably. You want to withdraw your offer of marriage?"

"Not on your life." He snuggled her close again. "What about Australia?"

"I think I could get you a position on this dig. It could be our honeymoon trip. We could get our own boat when this trip is over."

"Some honeymoon. I had it more in mind to be alone."

He winked at her, and her face grew hot. "We might be able to squeeze in a few days like that."

"When would you be able to find time to be married if you're leaving next week?"

She sighed. He was right. How could this all come together? He was going to have to stay here and she would have to go. "Other couples have survived a separation. I think we can, too."

"We can, but I don't want to." His scowl was coming back.

She smoothed his frown again. "We'll work it out somehow. I'll have a break at Christmas. Maybe we can get married then."

"Christmas? I don't want to wait that long."

"You sound like a little boy." She pinched his

cheeks. "Little Simon, be patient. We've got a lot to figure out."

"I'll try," he murmured from her hair again.

"We're docking," she told him. "Better go get your sieves."

"Come with me. I don't want you out of my sight."

Simon whistled as he jogged across the boatyard. He held on to Wynne's hand. Being with her gave him such a sense of completion. The problems of yesterday seemed to slide off his back with her at his side.

"I left the sieves in the office."

"There they are." Wynne stooped to pick them up where he'd left them by the door to his office.

"Let me get them. They're heavy." He'd built the sieves from window screen and pieces of two-by-fours. He picked them up and set them back down on a chair. "Wait, I need to get another cell phone. We have a spare somewhere." His cell phone was long gone after their ordeal yesterday.

He riffled through his desk. Not there. "Maybe it's in Brian's office."

"I'll look." Wynne went across the hall to his cousin's office. Simon followed her.

"It looks like a nor'easter blew through here." Wynne had a bewildered look on her face like she didn't know where to begin to look.

"No kidding." Simon stepped around an erasable board with indecipherable scribbles on it. He brushed too close to a stack of papers that was perched precariously on Brian's desk. The papers tumbled to the floor.

"Great. We don't have time for this." Simon was tempted to just leave them to Brian to pick up.

"I'll get them. You look for the phone." Wynne knelt and began to gather the papers together.

He went to the desk and pulled out the lap drawer. "Here's the phone," Simon called out. He checked the charge then put it in his pocket.

Wynne was frowning as she scanned a paper she'd picked up. "I thought you said the boatyard was struggling. It sure shouldn't be having any financial struggles with this kind of sale."

"What are you talking about?" He squatted beside her. She handed him the paper. It was from Laughton Cruise lines. He scanned it, but it took a few moments for the words to sink in. The company wanted to buy ten boats from Lassiter's. The figure they were paying made Simon blink.

"Fifty million dollars. No way."

"You didn't know anything about this?" Wynne asked.

Simon shook his head. "Brian never said a word. This talks about some kind of new innovation."

"Why would he keep this from you?" Wynne's voice was tentative, as though she were afraid of the answer.

Simon folded the paper and put it in his pocket. "I think I'll ask him." Anger overshadowed the trepidation he felt. He didn't want to examine what this meant, didn't want to feel as betrayed as he did.

"Simon, could this have anything to do with Jerry's death? Is this the same boat?"

"No, it sounds like it's something even bigger."

"Does Brian do all the designs?"

"Yes, all of it."

"Did you ever notice any jealousy between him and Jerry?"

Simon nodded slowly. "Jerry overshadowed everyone. Every girlfriend Brian had in their teen years, Jerry took eventually."

Wynne squeezed his hand. "Does he harbor bad feelings against you?"

"I don't think so. We've always been like brothers." He returned the pressure of her fingers. "Let's go talk to him. I think we're jumping to conclusions here."

"I hope so," Wynne said, following him to the door.

The boat engine was idling when they stepped back on deck. "Don't say anything yet," Simon cautioned Wynne. "Let me think about how to approach him."

She nodded, but her eyes were shadowed. Simon figured she was already convicting Brian, but he couldn't believe his cousin would do something like that.

He felt the crackle of the paper in his pocket, and it reminded him that something was amiss. It wasn't easy to explain away such a huge boat deal. Every time he tried to add it up, he kept coming up with a conclusion he couldn't bear.

He suddenly realized they were far from shore. Maybe he should wait to confront Brian until there were people around. Just in case he'd had something to do with the attempts on their lives. He wanted to discount the very notion that his cousin might want to harm him, but the ugly suspicion wouldn't go away.

"Here we are," Brian called. He cut the engine and lowered the anchor.

Simon looked at Wynne. If they went down, Brian would be left up here alone. He could leave them or sabotage them in some way. He saw the same fear in her eyes. There was no help for it. He would have to talk to Brian now. Better to do that than to dive and worry about what was happening on the surface.

He stepped closer to his cousin. "Brian, I need to talk to you."

Brian pushed his hair out of his eyes. "What's up?" He pointed to the sky. "This good weather isn't supposed to last. We'd better get down there and see what's happened."

"We will. But I have a question first." Simon pulled the letter from his pocket and opened it. "Can you explain this?"

Brian's eyes widened when he saw what was in Simon's hand. "Were you snooping in my office?" He went white, and his mouth was tight.

"Not really. I knocked off a stack of papers. This was in it." Simon held the paper away when Brian tried to snatch it. "When were you going to tell me about this? Why did you need my money with this kind of sale going through?"

"I needed some new equipment," Brian said, thrusting out his jaw.

Simon glanced at the letter and saw something he'd missed before. "The date is before Jerry died. Did he know about it?"

Brian put his hand in his pocket and pulled out a tiny pistol. The dark, round hole was small, but Simon knew it was deadly. "I'm sorry, Simon, but it has to be this way."

"You killed your own brother?" Simon still couldn't believe it. He glanced at Wynne then moved slightly in front of her to shield her with his body.

"I'd had it," Brian said bitterly. "Do you have any idea what it was like to live in his shadow? And Rhonda was the last straw. I thought she was the one until Jerry moved in once again. And when I came up with this new boat design, he was crowing about how rich he was going to be. Off *my* work, my designs. I couldn't take any more."

"I understand that," Simon said softly. "Did you try to kill us, too?"

"I didn't want to." When Simon shifted, Brian moved the gun so it was aimed at Wynne. "Don't try anything, Simon, or I'll have to shoot your pretty girlfriend."

Simon froze. "Put the gun down, Brian, and we can talk about this."

"Too late for talk." He smiled but there was no mirth in his face.

"We're no threat to you," Simon said, holding his hands out with the palms up.

"With you gone, the entire business is mine. I won't

have to live in anyone's shadow ever again." Brian's face hardened. "No more talk. It's time for you both to go diving."

TWENTY-THREE

"I'm not going in," Wynne said. She crossed her arms over her chest. "You're going to have to shoot me."

"I can do that," Brian warned.

"If you do, it will clearly be murder. You don't want that. That's why you've tried to dispose of us with accidents. The sheriff will know where to look if we turn up with bullet holes in our heads."

"You won't turn up." Brian smirked and his eyes were hard. "All I have to do is weight your bodies and dispose of you someplace where you'll never be found."

"But we *might* be found. Superior is capricious. A storm could toss up our bodies when you least expect it, just like it did with Jerry and Amanda."

Brian hesitated. "Maybe. But I'll do what I have to. Now get in the water."

He shot over Wynne's head, and it ruffled her hair as it passed. She flinched and took a step back.

"He's serious," Simon said.

"Move," Brian commanded. "Into the water, or the next shot goes through your forehead."

Wynne bit her lip. They had their dry suits on so the cold wouldn't kill them right away. They'd last a couple of hours until they'd need to warm up. She began to pray as she adjusted her mask and mouth-piece. Maybe they could make a determined effort to swim to safety.

"No. Take off the suit," Brian said.

"It won't look natural," Simon pointed out. "The sheriff will know we wouldn't go diving without our suits."

"I'll tell him we forgot them. He'll buy it since we lost the boat and equipment. Take them off." His voice was inflexible.

There went that idea. Wynne peeled her suit off. At least they had their oxygen. But it wouldn't do them much good if hypothermia got them. She went into the water, and Simon joined her. The cold immediately tightened her muscles.

Brian leaned on the railing but kept the gun trained on them. "Hypothermia is a great way to go." His tone was conversational. "It's fast and efficient."

Wynne glared at him. "Before we die, I'm going to go down and see the site one last time. I want to see if the storm buried it again." She didn't dare just dive without telling him what she was doing. She didn't want him to shoot at her or Simon.

Brian shrugged. "Suit yourself. The cold will just

take you faster. It's colder the farther down you go. But Simon stays here. If you don't come up in fifteen minutes, I shoot him."

Wynne had an idea. She glanced at Simon, adjusted her mouthpiece and dove. She kicked hard, willing her muscles to stay warm and limber. Angling her body for maximum velocity, she swam to the bottom of the lake.

The cold pierced her skin like tiny darts. She needed some kind of weapon. Her fingers were quickly turning numb, but she scrabbled through the muck at the bottom of the lake in search of something she could use. There was nothing. The storm had buried much of what they'd excavated.

Her fingers closed on a rock. She had a pretty good arm. The rock was nearly perfectly round, like a baseball. She'd have only one shot. Tucking it in the back of her swimsuit, she swam back to the surface.

Her head broke the water, and she spit her mouthpiece out. "It's all gone," she said. "The storm buried it again."

"Too bad you won't have an opportunity to dig it up again." Brian gestured with the gun. "Show me your hands."

Glad she'd assumed he'd ask, she held up both palms. "What did you think I had? No spearguns down there."

Brian laughed. "I like you, Wynne. I'm sorry you have to die."

"I wish I could say the same about you," she retorted.

His smile died. "If you'd had to live like I did all my life, you'd understand."

"Revenge is never worth it," Wynne said. "You have to answer for yourself before God."

"I'm not in the mood for a sermon," he said sharply. He glanced at his watch. "Getting warm yet?"

"Not so you'd notice." Wynne's teeth began to chatter. She glanced at Simon. He moved closer and put his arm around her waist.

"I don't think so." Brian wagged the gun at them. "No sense in dragging out the torture. You'll get cold quicker apart. You move over that way, Simon."

"No." Simon said, pulling Wynne closer. "If we're going to die, the least you can do is let us go together. Wynne agreed to marry me."

"I figured it was just a matter of time." Brian's eyes narrowed. "Maybe it will be my turn with everyone out of the way. I've seen the way women fawn over men with money. I'll be wealthy beyond my wildest dreams. I will be able to have my pick of women."

"Money doesn't solve all your problems," Simon said.

His lips were blue, and Wynne could feel him shivering. She reached behind her and dug out the rock she'd picked up. She grabbed his hand that was on her waist under the water and guided it to the rock so he could see what she had planned. He went rigid and looked at her from the corner of his eye.

"Maybe not, but I'm going to find out." Brian smiled.

Simon let go of her waist and began to move toward the boat. Wynne followed.

"What are you doing?" Brian called out shrilly.

"We're coming aboard. We're not going to just wait and let the water kill us." Simon reached the ladder and grasped it.

Wynne tensed, her fingers tightening on the rock. She'd reached the bow of the boat and grabbed hold to brace herself against it. Praying for God to guide her aim in spite of the numbness in her fingers, she tensed and got ready.

Brian leaned over the railing and aimed the gun at Simon. "Get back or I'll shoot."

With Brian's attention on Simon, she had a clear shot. *Help me, God.* She steadied herself with her left hand and aimed with her right. The rock left her fingers and sailed through the air. It struck Brian squarely on the wrist. The gun flew out of his hand and into the water.

He shouted and reached after it, nearly toppling into the water with the gun. Simon lumbered up the ladder, his movements slow from the onset of hypothermia. Brian rushed forward to grapple with him.

Wynne could barely feel her fingers, but she reached up and grasped the railing. She didn't think there was any way she could haul herself up from the water in her weakened state, but she had to help Simon or they were both dead.

She dug her toes into the hull of the boat. Her feet slipped off, but she tried again, seeking a small indentation she could wedge her toes into. Grunting and pulling, she finally managed to tug herself onto the deck. She stood outside the railing. Now all she had to do was swing her body over into the boat.

She teetered on the edge, almost too weary to make a move. Grunts and curses emanated from Brian as he struggled to toss Simon back into the water. Wynne sucked in a breath and watched the deadly confrontation for a moment. She could see Simon was barely hanging on. She had to do something.

With the last ounce of her strength, she clambered over the railing and at last stood swaying on the deck. She looked around wildly for a weapon. The sieves! She rushed forward and grabbed up the heavy metal sieve. It was all she could do to raise it over her head.

Shrieking, she tottered forward and brought it crashing down on Brian's head. He went down like a pile of rune stones. Wynne grabbed Simon's hand, and he fell forward onto the deck. She knelt and rolled him over.

"My girl, the Valkyrie," he said. He stood and pulled her into an embrace. "You sounded like a Norse warrior when you yelled. It was enough to curdle my blood." He prodded Brian with his foot. "He's out cold."

"Thank the Lord," Wynne said, drawing in a deep breath. The tension began to ease from her shoulders, but she was still shaking, both from reaction and from the cold.

"I'll call the Coast Guard." He headed toward the ship-to-shore phone.

Wynne went to the cabinets and dragged out some blankets. She put one around herself and draped one over Simon's shoulders. He shot her a grateful smile.

Wynne could hardly believe it was over. She glanced to where Brian still lay on the deck. Such a sweet exterior hiding such a black soul. He had so much potential, too. Such a brilliant designer, and he threw away his bright future for money.

But hadn't she been teetering on doing that very thing? Oh, not for money, but for fame in her field. She'd been stressing about contracts and her career, when the really important things in life were relationships and people. Instead of asking what God would have her do, she'd been trying to figure it out on her own, as if it all depended on her, when in reality, God was the designer of her life.

Simon put down the phone. "The Coast Guard is on its way." He slipped his arm around her shoulders. "You okay?"

"I'm fine. Starting to warm up."

"Me, too. But remind me to let you teach our kids how to throw. You nailed that gun dead-on."

She laughed. "We make a team that is pretty hard to beat."

Brian stirred. "I'd better tie him up." Simon grabbed a hank of rope and tied Brian's hands behind him. "That should hold him."

Brian groaned and rolled over onto his back. His

eyelids fluttered. He tried to sit up and moaned again when he realized he was bound. His shoulders slumped.

The sound of a boat growled in the distance. "Here comes the Coast Guard," Wynne said.

Brian's eyes opened wide. "Let me go," he begged.

"You know I can't do that," Simon said.

"It's my word against yours." Brian jutted his chin forward.

"Against both of ours," Wynne pointed out.

Brian staggered to his feet and plunged toward the railing. "Stop him!" Wynne shouted.

Brian barreled over the railing and splashed into the water. He sank without another sound.

The sun was setting in the west by the time the Coast Guard divers recovered Brian's body. Wynne was more than ready to head back to shore, but she and Simon wanted to wait until they knew it was all over. Until the body was recovered, there was always the chance that Brian had survived.

Simon watched silently as they loaded his cousin's body. Wynne stood in the circle of his arms—the place she now felt most secure. She leaned back against his chest. "I'm sorry about Brian, Simon. You have to be devastated."

He grew rigid, and his arms slackened. She felt cold when he turned away. He hit his fist against the railing. "It's so senseless." His voice was tight and harsh. "I would have done anything to help him. Why didn't he come to me if he thought Jerry was taking advantage of him?"

Wynne heard the raw pain under the anger in his voice. She touched his forearm. "It's not your fault, Simon. I know you like to take care of everyone, but you can't. Brian was an adult. He's responsible for his own choices, not you."

She felt him flinch, then he turned his head and gazed into her eyes. Her eyes filled with tears at the suffering in his face. "I'm sorry, Simon."

"I know." He sounded hoarse. Drawing her into his arms again, he rested his chin on top of her head. "I don't know what I'd do if you weren't here. It would be pretty unbearable."

"I'm not going anywhere."

"What about Australia?"

"I'm leaving that up to you. What do you think is the right thing for us to do?" She could get into this passing the buck, she thought. She trusted Simon's judgment so completely, and it felt comforting to turn things over to him.

"Oh, sure, make me decide."

She heard the smile in his voice as she snuggled against his chest. "You're going to be the spiritual leader. So lead on."

He gave a heavy sigh, and her heart skipped. Was he sorry he'd asked her to marry him? She tipped her head back and looked up into his face. "What's wrong?"

"You need to honor your commitment to the

contract," he said quietly. "But I don't have to like it." He puffed his cheeks out and exhaled. "This being responsible to God for the right decisions is a bummer. It was more fun to growl about you leaving me."

She didn't know whether to be happy or sad. But she knew it was right. "I'll miss you," she muttered.

"I'm coming with you if you can land me a contract, too. If you can't, I'll wait patiently."

"You willing to part with a little cold, hard cash? Our dig is operating on a shoestring budget. Offer a grant, and he'll be even more likely to agree."

"I can do that," he said. "But there's one more big problem we have to discuss."

"Uh-oh, that sounds ominous." Was he going to ask her to give up everything and stay here once the Australia contract was fulfilled? If he did, could she agree?

He gripped her shoulders and scowled. "It's about our past."

"Our past?" Their present had consumed so much of her thoughts, she'd forgotten they'd known each other once upon a time in their childhood.

"It's about that thing you overheard," he began.

A smile played at her lips. "I won't say a word."

"It's okay if you do," he said. "In fact, I've decided I'm not hiding anything. You can call me anything you want."

A chuckle built in her throat. "You might reconsider. Do you remember that nickname?"

He groaned. "How could I forget?"

Wynne well remembered the day herself. She'd

stood with three other girls behind a tree and listened to Simon's girlfriend of the hour break up with him. When Simon realized he'd been overheard, he'd been humiliated as only a seventeen-year-old boy can be.

"Kiss me, Woobie," she said, pulling his lips down to meet hers.

Dear Reader,

Lake Superior has a wonderful mystique. Vast, cold and deadly, it's the perfect backdrop for this final story in the Great Lakes Legends series. In Ojibwa legend, the Thunderbird is said to flap its wings and stir up the ferocious storms that sweep over Superior, and there are storms aplenty in *Stormcatcher*—both dangerous ones and romantic ones.

I've been fascinated with my research into the legends of the Great Lakes. I hope you enjoy the final excursion!

I love hearing from my readers. Visit me at www.colleencoble.com and e-mail me at colleen@colleencoble.com.

Colleen Rhoads

Love Inspired®
SUSPENSE

TITLES AVAILABLE NEXT MONTH

Don't miss these two stories in March

THROUGH THE FIRE by Sharon Mignerey
Faith at the Crossroads

Firefighter Lucia Vance felt the heat when she was suspended after suspicious chemicals were found at the site of a blaze she fought. With an accusation of wrongdoing hanging over her and the real culprit determined to harm her, fellow firefighter Rafael Wright's belief in her innocence was her lifeline—and possibly her only hope to survive.

WHEN SILENCE FALLS by Shirlee McCoy
Part of the LAKEVIEW miniseries

Piper Sinclair's plans to spend her summer doing research for a book were complicated when she witnessed a kidnapping, becoming a target herself. Crime scene photographer Cade Macalister knew his friend's little sister couldn't face the dangerous assailant by herself, so he was determined to protect her—whether she liked it or not.

LISCNM0206